PERMANENT VACANCY

KATY LEE

LOVE INSPIRED BOOKS

ISBN-13: 978-0-373-67687-3

Permanent Vacancy

Copyright © 2013 by Katy Lee

All rights reserved. Except for use in any review, the reproduction or utilization of this work in whole or in part in any form by any electronic, mechanical or other means, now known or hereafter invented, including xerography, photocopying and recording, or in any information storage or retrieval system, is forbidden without the written permission of the publisher, Harlequin Enterprises Limited, 225 Duncan Mill Road, Don Mills, Ontario M3B 3K9, Canada.

This is a work of fiction. Names, characters, places and incidents are either the product of the author's imagination or are used fictitiously, and any resemblance to actual persons, living or dead, business establishments, events or locales is entirely coincidental.

This edition published by arrangement with Harlequin Books S.A.

For questions and comments about the quality of this book please contact us at Customer_eCare@Harlequin.ca.

® and TM are trademarks of the publisher. Trademarks indicated with ® are registered in the United States Patent and Trademark Office, the Canadian Trade Marks Office and in other countries.

www.Harlequin.com

⊕ HARLEQUIN® LOVE INSPIRED® SUSPENSE

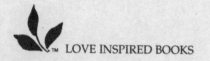

LOVE INSPIRED BOOKS

ISBN-13: 978-0-373-67687-3

Permanent Vacancy

Copyright © 2015 by Katherine Lee

www.Harlequin.com

Printed in U.S.A.

Those who trust in themselves are fools,
but those who walk in wisdom are kept safe.
–Proverbs 28:26

Finally, brothers and sisters, rejoice! Strive for full
restoration, encourage one another, be of one mind, live in
peace. And the God of love and peace will be with you.
–2 Corinthians 13:11

To my husband, Bill. I love you and I thank God for you.

Acknowledgments

I am a great believer that it takes a village
to publish a book. First and foremost, it takes readers.
I'm so grateful to you all. Thank you for picking my book up
and not putting it down. Thank you for your dedication
to the Love Inspired series. I write for you.

I'd also like to thank David Bond, electrician and author,
for helping me put a little zap in the book.
I'm usually a safety-first kind of gal,
so thank you for the help with deadly hazards.

I'm so blessed to have a family that cheers me on.
Not a word would be written without your support and
help. Thank you, guys, for understanding a closed door
doesn't mean I don't love you. It means I love you enough
to show you what going after your dreams looks like.
And that it's worth it.

And finally, thank you, Emily Rodmell.
With you as my editor, my writing
has your special touch that makes it shine.

ONE

Three things stopped Gretchen Bauer dead in her tracks: the smashed pots of her morning glory seedlings splattering her porch steps, the Public Hearing Notice, aka Notice of Betrayal, nailed to her door frame, and the paint-chipped front door of her old Victorian standing ajar.

Someone had been here—and still might be.

Broken terra-cotta pieces crunched beneath her sneaker treads as she took the first tentative step up. The new beginnings of her signature bed-and-breakfast flowers were strewn about the landing, their futures dashed in an instant.

A sign of her own future?

The answer awaited her at the door.

Her gaze fell to the shadows of the rough interior of her house that she could see through the crack.

Then she saw again the white piece of paper posted to the door's right. Its crisp black type stated details of a town meeting set to discuss the future of her renovation of the abandoned home she'd recently purchased.

But she knew what the message really meant.

No matter what she did to move forward in her life, a certain someone would always yank her back. The words read Public Hearing Notice. They may as well have said You Will Never Be Free.

Gretchen craved freedom more than air, and since she was asthmatic, that said a lot. But in four weeks, she would hang her own message from her lamppost. The shingle for her business would read The Morning Glory B&B, Stepping Stones Island, Maine.

The true meaning behind it would read, *I'm free.*

From then on she would be free to make her own choices without asking for permission. She would be free to pick her friends without obtaining background checks and approval. She would be free of being manipulated by words— and actions.

The stinging memory of where she had felt his last action spread across her cheek. She touched it protectively and vowed it would never happen again.

"Welcome home, love," a male's voice called from behind her.

Gretchen inhaled and whipped around, her

hands raised in front of her face and ready to fight her bully. How dare he—

A huge video camera closed in on her instead, catching her off guard. Gretchen shrank back a step, unable to see who stood behind the huge piece of equipment. "What's going on?" She changed her battling fists to palms straight up to say *Stand back.* "Who are you? This is private property."

"You invited us, love. Don't you remember?" An Irishman's voice pulled her attention away from the camera and down to where he stood on the walkway. "Allow me to introduce myself. I'm C—"

"Colm McCrae," she answered for him on an exhale of relief. Her hands dropped with her shoulders. She immediately thanked God that it was he and not— Never mind. "Of course I remember," Gretchen replied. "You're the host of the cable television show *Rescue to Restoration.* I did invite you to help with my renovation. Thank you so much for coming."

She put her hand over her chest. "You just surprised me. I wasn't expecting you. I was told you weren't arriving until late this afternoon."

"Aye," he answered in his suave Irish accent that brought him his fame on his home improvement show, especially with the lady viewers. "My cameraman and I rented a boat. We came over from the mainland on our own to get started. It's right deadly, don't you think?"

"Deadly?"

"Oh, apologies, Dublin lingo. I meant to say 'fantastic news.' Aye? What do you say you give me a gander around the place?" He stepped up onto the porch. His long legs skipped the two stairs of broken pots with ease as he pressed in close to her. She stepped back again and hit the door frame.

Then she noticed the camera moved in, too.

Gretchen looked in every direction, unsure of where to rest her eyes. The presence of a camera brought on a whole new feeling of intrusion she hadn't counted on when she applied for the show to assist her in her rehab. At the time, it felt like a smart idea, but right now smiling for the camera didn't seem possible. She was still too tense from finding her home vandalized and had barely caught her breath. Plus, this program host came across as a little domineering. She hadn't expected that, either.

But then, after eight years of being with someone who dominated her whole existence, she might be judging this TV personality too soon.

"You want a tour *now*?" Gretchen grappled for words while acclimating herself to her guests. "I didn't expect you to be filming today. May I have a moment to prepare, please?" She put her hand up in front of her face and used her mass of curls to hide behind.

"The light looks good on you, Goldie. It would be a shame to waste it."

Colm's sudden nickname for her unnerved her further. It made her think of that other smooth talker in her life.

Check that: old life.

"Gretchen," she corrected the host and turned from the lens in her face to see him step close to her. He was more real than he'd ever appeared, even in high definition, in her living room. She lifted her head, then lifted it some more to meet his eyes. He towered nearly a foot over her five feet.

Just breathe, she told herself, but when she opened her mouth, Colm McCrae asked, "Did the public notice bring you a wee bit of bad news?" His accent slowed her understanding, although the reddish streaks glinting through his wavy chestnut hair also distracted her. That and the concern filling his blue puppy-dog eyes. Was the concern legit? She shook her head to clear it.

It didn't matter.

"Trouble? No," she answered. Her days of trouble had ended when she'd sent a certain heavy-fisted deputy in the sheriff's department packing. "Just a little misunderstanding with the town. I'll get it taken care of—" Her voice trailed off as she noticed Colm and the cameraman pressing in even closer. The two seemed to work in sync to invade her private space.

A red flag hoisted high and waved in her mind's eye. Had she escaped one bully only to sign on with another? She'd send them right away if that was the case.

But renovations took money, and Gretchen had already spent every dime she'd earned from waitressing and doing odd jobs around the island to buy the house and to update the plumbing and electricity. She had to if she wanted to live here. To turn away the crew would mean returning to her waitressing life and serving her ex when he came in for his weekly bratwurst at her mother's German restaurant. The thought of her old puppet master winning caused her breath to catch and wheeze. The man wasn't even here and he still tainted her dreams from the crew's first take. She reached into her jeans pocket for her inhaler and took a quick pull of the medicine to open her lungs. Disgust filled her at this ailment that weakened her.

"Asthma?" the host asked.

Gretchen nodded and pocketed the inhaler behind her. She straightened her pink short-sleeved polo with conviction. "I'll be fine now," she stated. Billy would no longer be her puppet master, she determined again. And the television crew would be staying.

But that also meant showing them they couldn't push her around. "Where is your director, Troy Mullen?" she demanded. "I met him three months ago when he visited the island to interview me. He assured me he would be a part of the production from day one."

"He'll be here later with the rest of the crew and supplies," Colm answered.

"Then you can turn off your camera and wait for him."

"No can do, ma'am." A black-bearded face popped out from behind the camera. It was her first glimpse of the cameraman. He looked nice enough with his round head and big cheeks, even if his words weren't what she wanted to hear. "You signed the release and accepted the terms. We determine what to film."

"Terms?" A sudden flash of the stack of papers she signed: lots of liability or lack thereof on her side. The camera lens reflected her wavering image. As she stared at herself she watched resignation take over. She'd have to get used to it, beginning now. "Yes, I remember. Let's just start over, then." She looked to the host. "Mr. McCrae, would you like that tour now?"

"Call me Colm." The host leaned in even more. The red flag waved again. Then Gretchen saw that he wore a small black microphone clipped to the lapel of his denim shirt. A sudden realization hit her. Her voice wouldn't be recorded properly if she wasn't speaking into a microphone. That had to be why he stood so close.

Gretchen almost laughed aloud at her misplaced paranoia. What was wrong with her? Just because one man in her life had been a bully didn't make all men bullies.

"Actually, Gretchen," Colm said, "I'd love to hear more about this town meeting. A bit of tension in the town about a B&B opening on its island could be grand for ratings, wouldn't you say, Nate?"

The cameraman, who could only be Nate, grunted. "I don't think that's what the boss has in mind. He'll want something more exciting than a town meeting to spike ratings."

Gretchen searched Colm McCrae's face. Nate's was hidden again behind his equipment. "More exciting? Ratings?" she said. "Please don't tell me you're looking to fabricate a problem just so you can spike your rankings. I thought this show was about educating people to renovate their homes. I thought you were above such manipulating tactics."

Nate and Colm laughed, Colm's more rich than the cameraman's. "I'm not sure there's a show out there that isn't concerned with ratings, Miss Bauer."

"Well, there's no big story to tell here, so you can get that out of your head. Now, do you want the tour, or don't you?"

Colm leaned down mere inches from her face. He put his arm over her shoulder. She felt his cool, minty breath on the same cheek that held a memory of a hot, searing pain. She held stock-still and gave nothing away. The door squeaked behind her as Colm pushed it wider and said, "After you, love."

Gretchen swung around to enter, welcoming the space between them. Colm's boots hit her wooden floors with heavy clunks as he followed her in. She flinched with every stomp, still a bit unnerved.

He passed her and surveyed the foyer with a growing frown on his clean-shaven face. His gaze fell on the pitiful staircase and stopped. Where once a grand flight of stairs had curved up to the second-floor balcony, now only stair treads remained, the railing gone.

"The door needs a little oil and it'll be right as rain," Colm announced. "But the interior is a whole other story. Three weeks to completion? We won't have the house done this side of Christmas." He covered his mic and whispered, "Troy's lost his mind."

Gretchen's ears perked to Colm McCrae's last words. Not so much the words but how he said them.

He'd dropped his Irish accent.

"Wait," she interrupted. "You're not really Irish?"

He swung a quick look at her. "Of course I'm Irish." He flashed a smile of straight white teeth. "You want to kiss me?"

"What? No!" She shook her head to clear the image he'd conjured up in her mind. "I know I just heard you speak with no accent. Or at least not an Irish one."

Colm's grin deepened. "Good catch. I suppose I slipped. Don't tell anyone. I have an image to uphold." At his wink Gretchen pressed her lips together. The past eight years of her life were about upholding a man's image. She wasn't about to start again for another, not even the famous Colm McCrae.

She folded her arms. "I can't believe this. You're nothing but a big phony."

Colm's smile evaporated. "Don't worry about the tour, Miss Bauer. We have a lot of work to do. I'll inspect the place today myself and decide what projects to start with. You're welcome to check in periodically."

"Check in? Mr. McCrae, I live here."

"You live here? Kind of dangerous, don't you think? Especially with your asthma."

"My asthma is under control as long as I have my inhaler, not that it's any of your concern."

"Does this place even have running water and electricity?"

"Surprise, surprise, Mr. McCrae, I not only have good ears, but I'm also pretty handy." She wished she could have handled the whole renovation, but that would have taken years, and money she didn't have.

"Pretty." He looked right at her. "Aye, I see that."

Gretchen opened her mouth at his gall.

He held up his hands. "Look, Goldie, I'll admit I'm impressed with your skills, but even still, it's not customary to have the home owner on-site during renovating and shooting. It's a work zone. It could be right dangerous. Murder, really. Troy would never allow—"

"Too bad, because I'm not going anywhere. I have a vested interest in the outcome of this project. This is my home, but in four weeks, it will also be my business and my future."

Colm sputtered, "Love, I hate to tell you, but there's no way you're opening in four weeks."

"Your director promised me three. I'm holding you all to it. Now, if you'll follow me upstairs, I'll show you the guest rooms you're to start with. Once you're finished upstairs I can begin decorating."

"Seems like you have things all planned out."

"I'm in charge now, if that's what you mean." Gretchen stepped past him. "This way, Mr. McCr— Aaah!" Splintering wood smothered her scream. One moment she stood in her foyer, the next, her floor swallowed her whole.

"Gretchen!" Colm dropped to his knees and approached the gap in the floor where less than a second ago the home owner with her mass of golden curls fell through. "Are you all right?"

"McCrae, Irish accent," Nate said from behind. A quick glimpse showed the camera still rolling. Colm clenched his fists and jaw. The show was the last thing he cared about at the moment. Nate's raised bushy eyebrows reminded him what he cared about didn't matter. He wasn't the boss.

"Goldie, love, are you all right?" He pushed out the thick brogue, hating it more now than ever—but not as much as the fact that she didn't respond. *Please, God, be with the young woman.*

Colm peered past the broken boards into a dark and dank cellar. His eyes adjusted quickly enough to capture Gretchen lying right below. She didn't look to have fallen far, from what he could tell by the low basement ceiling, but he couldn't be sure. "Our home owner has taken a tumble through her foyer floor," Colm said, trying to play his part for the camera, when really he wanted to jump in after her. "This could be right serious and just woeful. She's not responding to my call."

Colm stood abruptly, knowing Nate would follow on his heels. After two years of working together on the show, they'd learned each other's movements, even though nothing like this had ever happened on location. Sure, there were mishaps, but those were minor or typically used for commercial breaks. Viewers liked the excitement of staying tuned in to find out what happened. And when the accident had been remedied and all was well again, they sat back on their couches and watched on. Minor mishaps worked great, but a serious injury could ruin him. It could send him back to the place he never wanted to go again.

But it would be so much worse for Gretchen.

Colm ran to the back of the house and located the door to the basement. His boots hit the stairs in a rapid cadence that matched his heartbeat. What would he find below? Her neck twisted in an unnatural way?

Please, God, let her be well, he prayed again.

Be with me so I can help her. A twinge of guilt gripped him when he realized he had been worried about his job a moment ago. Gretchen Bauer could have broken her neck in the fall, and he was worried about being fired. What kind of person did that make him?

As if he didn't know.

Nate followed behind, his camera light illuminating the dirt floor as Colm's feet hit the compacted earth. He had been correct about the low ceiling. The way he had to crouch told him less than six feet stood between floor and ceiling. At least it was a short fall. *Thank You, Lord, for old houses.* He ran toward where Gretchen lay.

A groan came from that direction. She was alive. Colm allowed a little relief to come, but only a little. She could still be quite hurt. He prepared himself for the worst and pulled his phone from his pocket, ready to call 911. "Gretchen, hold still," he called.

The camera light made finding her easy in the dark. He reached her as she pulled herself up to a sitting position. "Don't move!" he shouted and knelt to stop her. "You shouldn't move until emergency personnel have had a chance to check you out. I'm calling 911."

"No." Gretchen grabbed his hand, her touch not delicate as he'd imagined, but rough and strong. She turned away from the camera's light, putting half her pale features into the darkness. "Don't call the sheriff's office," she said. "I just had the wind knocked out of me."

"Do you need your inhaler?"

She reached behind her, pulling out a smashed container.

"I'm calling," he announced, his finger about to hit the number 9.

"Please don't," she whispered. The camera wouldn't have picked her voice up without her hooked to a microphone, but Colm heard it loud and clear.

For some reason the idea of notifying the sheriff's office scared her more than her fall, more than the inability to breathe.

"Are you positive? Sometimes we don't feel an injury until later."

"I'm fine."

Colm studied her for a moment in silence, searching for any injury she might be hiding or not know of yet. She flexed her shoulders and moved her head a bit to demonstrate that she was uninjured. Colm's own adrenaline sank back to a normal level and when he looked up at the camera, he saw it continued to roll. Nate had filmed the whole scene. Colm wasn't surprised. He knew Troy would expect it. The director was sure to eat this incident up. Probably use it for pre-ads to the airing to create some excitement for the upcoming episode. Colm also knew what the director expected of him. Troy would want him to wrap up this scene with a nice little bow. The fact that Gretchen was unhurt meant Colm could continue doing his job. He could now add a little of the humor he was famous for without feeling guilty.

Colm grabbed a piece of floorboard that had come down with Gretchen. He lifted it to the camera. "I don't know about you, but I can say for sure it wasn't our home owner's weight that sent her through the floor. I've seen more meat on a chicken's forehead, if you're following my drift. I'll also say her decision to call *Rescue to Restoration* may have saved her life if the condition of these floorboards means anyth—"

Colm stared at the board in his hand, unable to continue with his monologue. He may be just a host for the show, but long before his time in front of the camera, he had spent many hours beside his da in his woodshop. Colm studied the wood.

Sharp angles, rough edges. Too perfect to be a break.

He looked over the piece at Gretchen Bauer. She dropped her gaze to her hands in her lap. Was this why she didn't want the sheriff's office notified? Did she wonder the same thing he did? Or did she already know the answer to his unasked question?

"This was no accident, Miss Bauer, was it? Speak to me, Goldie. Who'd want'cha dead?"

TWO

"Dead?" Gretchen gasped. "Nobody wants me dead."

Do they?

No, of course not. She fought with the doubts that had appeared in her head the moment her back had come into abrupt contact with the dirt floor. "Why would you say such a thing?" Her words rose in defiance as she pushed her sore body up to stand, biting back the aches. "I've lived on Stepping Stones my whole life. The people here love me. They would never hurt me." The statement fell flat even to her ears.

"After seeing these boards *and* the public notice on your front door, I'd say not all of them love you. You've lived here long enough to make a few enemies, and one enemy is really all it takes to cut a few floorboards."

"How do you know they were cut? Unless..." A breath-halting realization struck her. "You cut them. That's why you know they were tampered with. You probably did this for your show. To up those ratings you were talking about, am I right?"

Please, let me be right.

"Now, wait just a second. You are way off. I would never—"

"You came inside before I returned home and set the scene up. I played right into your plan. Contrary to what people think around here, I do have a brain. I know when someone's playing me."

"Playing you? Why? Who played you before? Your islanders? The ones you say love you so much? I thought you just said none of them would ever hurt you. Perhaps you want to modify your words. Someone *has* messed with you. Am *I* right?"

Gretchen opened her mouth to deny it but in all honesty couldn't. But that didn't mean she would admit it. Never could she admit it to anyone.

Not when she'd let it happen.

But it didn't matter: Colm McCrae already knew. Maybe not all the details, but he knew. Shame doused her attempt to make sense of the situation. The fact was, when she fell through the floor, she had a good idea who had done this. But instead of admitting to knowing what her ex was capable of and his possible involvement in this incident, she was quick to find blame elsewhere. *Anywhere.* Even the crew that was here to help her get out from under Deputy Billy Baker's hold.

But why? Why couldn't Gretchen just say there was someone who'd want to hurt her and had?

Oh please, you know exactly why.

Deep down she wanted to believe she would never date a man capable of such a thing. Billy may have been controlling. He may have misused the word *love.* He may have gone above and beyond his duty to protect her by smothering her instead. But none of these things meant he would kill her.

But he had hit her.

Gretchen reached again for her right cheek. How could one slap have such a lasting and debilitating effect?

"You're right." She dropped her hand to her side. "There is someone who hurt me once. I can't say they did this, but I can say that's why you're here now—so I never have to depend on anyone again. I contacted *Rescue to Restoration* for more than a rehab. It's not only the house that's getting a rescue, it's me, too. And when you finish, and I open the front door to my first guests, it will be the beginning of a fully restored me. It will be the beginning of my new life."

Gretchen released a deep breath, wishing honesty came this easily with her family and friends. Maybe someday when she was stronger, after she'd proven she could succeed with not only the business, but also with the plans she made for her life, she would tell them, too. "Mr. McCrae, as you can see, we have a lot of work to do if we're going to reach our goal in only three weeks. Obviously, the person who did this wanted to halt the project at the get-go. So, what do you say? Can we show them they didn't win and get started?"

Colm's smile widened to deepen his famous dimples. Gretchen let a smile grow in return. Then again, she wasn't sure if she had any control over her lips at all. The man was gorgeous.

"I'm your man, Goldie, love." He lifted a hand and made a slicing action across his neck. "Cut. That was perfect, Gretchen. The viewers are going to love you."

"Cut?" she replied, stunned and confused at the same time. She felt her smile droop. The room darkened as Nate removed the camera from his shoulder and took the light with him toward the stairs. "Wait! This whole thing was filmed?" Her confession blared in her mind. The admission she had withheld from her family and friends would now be viewed by the whole country, the whole world, perhaps. But most definitely the island.

"Oh, no! You can't air what I said. Please!" She rushed out to follow Colm and Nate. They gave no response. "Please, listen to me. People around here won't understand."

"Terms, Miss Bauer," Nate reminded her. At the time she'd had no idea the show would be insensitive to her wishes. She should send them away. Risk a lawsuit if need be. Obviously, Billy had been right and she couldn't make a good decision to save her life. Calling the show could be the worst decision she'd ever made.

No. Dating him was.

And Billy would want her to second-guess any decision she made so that she would ultimately fail at this endeavor. Then she would fall right back into her old life, which included all of the ways he pulled her strings.

At the top of the stairs Nate looked back at Colm. "I'm heading to the bluffs for some stills for fillers while the light's good. Be back in an hour or so."

"Sounds good. I'm going to look around here for a while." All traces of the Irishman's accent were gone again as the two men carried on with business—as though her future mattered not at all.

"Mr. McCrae!" Gretchen yelled from the bottom of the stairs. He stopped on the top tread and looked over his shoulder. Even in the shadows she could see his perfectly sculpted eyebrows raised in question over the sleepy-eyed stare the camera and his fans loved so much. But Gretchen saw the real, ugly side of Colm McCrae, and as of this moment, he had lost a fan.

"You should know I'm nobody's puppet," she stated loud and clear. "Don't try that again. And I want this whole scene erased."

"Or what? You think you can rehab this place alone?"

She huffed at this egomaniac—even though her own mother had asked the same unsupportive question numerous times. "Not alone, Mr. McCrae. On my own," she shot back with all the vigor pent up from everyone's betrayal. "I will restore this place *on my own*. There's a difference."

He stood silently, chewing on the inside of his cheek. He gave a quick nod and started to walk away. Before he disappeared around the corner, he stopped. "I can't promise anything, but I'll see what I can do."

Gretchen stared up at the empty doorway. *See what he can do?* Wasn't he the host of the show? Didn't he have clout? It didn't make sense, unless…

Gretchen inhaled sharply.

It would seem she wasn't the only one who had a puppet master. Colm McCrae had to perform for one, too?

The metal tape measure zipped back into its case after Colm took a few quick measurements of the gaping hole in the foyer floor. He tossed it back into his bucket of tools, figuring he could repair the damage today before his crew and trailers arrived. He also figured Troy would be happy not to have it cut into the strict rehab schedule.

A schedule that didn't include stopping someone with murderous intent, but now just might.

Colm felt the edge of the rough-cut hole. His fingers came away with chewed sawdust. Whoever cut this had used the wrong size blade. Not that it mattered; Gretchen still fell through. It did the trick.

Her ashen face appeared in his mind.

Almost did the trick, if they were looking for death as the outcome. Would there be another attempt?

She'd told him someone had hurt her once. Once was one too many times in Colm's book, but also unrealistic. Most lowlifes came back for more. They thrived on the power they held over someone. Had her lowlife returned to strike again? She apparently didn't want anyone to know.

Textbook response.

Colm felt a deep irritation that had lived in him since he was a wee one. After his da's death, his mother had remarried a real bowsie of a man. Gil Griffin used his hands for things other than carpentry. Emily Griffin hid her bruises well.

What kind of bruises are you sportin', Gretchen?

The ceiling overhead creaked, stealing Colm's attention. Someone was upstairs. He'd just left Gretchen downstairs, and Nate had headed out the back door to walk the path to the cliff's edge for photos.

Colm pushed up from the floor and approached the first stair. He scanned the second-floor balcony for the visitor. Or perhaps it was the hole-cutter still at the scene of the crime, here to witness the outcome of his or her handiwork.

Colm clenched his fists before remembering his promise to God: no more fighting. The Dublin street fighter Colm McCrae was no more. God's saving grace made him a new creation, one who didn't use his fists to settle things. That was his stepfather's way. It didn't have to be his.

But that didn't mean he was going to invite the intruder for coffee. Or approach him or her unarmed.

Colm reached for the hammer in his tool belt. The tool's head was smooth from virtually no use, even though he'd carried it with him for the past two years as the show's host. It didn't matter that the belt was just for show; the tools attached were very real and would do well to strike fear and persuade minds. Colm balanced the weight of the hammer in his hand, testing its potential for use.

With no railing on the open side of the staircase, Colm stuck closer to the wall, each foot lightly placed and centered. Surprisingly the stairs remained quiet and held his weight well. Overall the house seemed sturdy. When he was down in the basement he'd noticed three-by-ten construction. Everything used to be so well built. Gretchen would have a fine home and establishment when the renovation was complete. That was, if she avoided the person who wanted to harm her.

Colm searched the top-floor hall as he approached the final step. The railing was intact here as it encased the hall. A sweep of his palm met smooth, strong mahogany. Beautifully carved spindles caught his eye for a split second, but they would have to wait for his adoration. The person behind one of the eight doors off the hall came first.

Colm stilled with a wall to his back. He listened for any sounds. All seemed quiet. Maybe he'd imagined the creaking floor before.

He heard a door close at his left.

No. Definitely not imagined.

Colm walked head-on to the back-left side door. He didn't wait to be surprised but barreled in at full force, hands and hammer raised.

A person with a mass of golden curls stopped him cold, hammer frozen in midstrike.

Gretchen shrank back as her arms flew to her face. Her mouth opened and Colm knew she was about to scream. He quickly lowered the hammer and closed in. "I'm so sorry," he assured her. "So, so sorry. I didn't mean to frighten you." He slowly replaced the hammer in its loop and raised his hands surrender-style. "See, I don't want to harm you."

Her face had drained of all color. She'd yet to scream, and that was when he noticed air was going in her mouth, but not coming out.

An asthma attack? But she wasn't wheezing. This was more like hyperventilating. But hyperventilating could lead to an asthma attack if not brought under control.

And with no inhaler since her fall, he couldn't let that happen.

Colm searched the box-filled room and found a battered chair. He lowered Gretchen gently into it. On his knees, he looked into her eyes.

"Goldie, breathe with me." He demonstrated a slow exhale and inhale. She seemed to be trying to match him, but unsuccessfully. "Try it. I promise it will work. Just follow my lead."

She didn't.

"Let's see, how about we try this? My ma used to hyperventilate and a sweet chewy always did the trick." Colm opened a compartment on his belt and withdrew some bubble gum. "I'm going to put this in your mouth. I want you to chew once and breathe out. Then chew again and breathe in. Can you do that?"

At her nod, he slowly placed the sweet gum on the tip of her tongue and mimicked a chew.

She did it, along with a short exhale. Slowly, her mind switched gears and she chewed again and again while breathing steadily in and out.

"That's right. Just grand." He beamed at her. When her breaths quieted down, he asked, "Better?"

She nodded, smiled weakly...then jumped from her chair. "Why would you scare the life out of me like that? You could have killed me if that went into an asthma attack." She scanned the corners of the room. "Wait. Please tell me I'm not going to find another one of your cameras in here."

"No cameras. And I said I was sorry. I had no idea you were in here, or even upstairs. I heard someone walking around and thought it might be the person who cut the floorboards. Honest. I had no idea it was you. How did you get up here, anyway? You never passed by me on the stairs."

Still dealing with the aftermath of her hyperventilation, Gretchen fell back into the chair like a rag doll. "Back staircase. There's a servants' house with a stairwell that connects to the second floor. I had just come through the door behind me when you—"

"You had just come through? You mean you weren't up here for a while? Like at least five minutes?"

She shook her head.

Colm looked back out toward the hall. He looked at the back entrance she had used. "And you didn't meet anyone in the back stairwell on your way up?"

"No."

"And there's no other way downstairs but by the two stairways?"

"No."

"Then I'd say someone else is still up here with us." He touched the handle of his hammer but paused before taking it out. "Stay here while I check it out."

She bounced back up. "No way. This is my house, and if someone's in here, I want to know who it is. Besides, you won't be able to identify the person—I will."

Her idea didn't sit well with him. She could have broken her neck once today. He didn't like her putting it out there again. He'd rather she leave the house while he searched it, but judging by the tilt of her chin, she wasn't going anywhere.

"Stay close, and if I tell you to run for the hills, you better leg it." Colm withdrew the hammer up and out of its loop again. Heading back out into the hall, he stopped at the first closed door and swung it wide. Empty, except for a bed and dresser placed against the far wall. Obviously Gretchen's makeshift room for the time being. He shut the door to move on, but a sound came from two doors down.

Colm brought his arm up to stop her. She didn't balk, which told him she'd heard it, too, and understood the danger of the situation. He made his way to the room, shoving the door wide.

Before he could say anything to the man standing there, Gretchen let out a quick gasp behind him and said, "Seriously? How could you?"

THREE

The picture before Gretchen was ludicrous. Len
Smith held a crowbar in his withered hand. The
ninety-five-year-old man could barely stand up
straight, never mind raise the tool above his
slumped head to fight Colm, who couldn't be
older than twenty-eight.

"Colm, put the hammer down," she instructed
the younger, very ruggedly strong man who was
no match for the elderly, declining one. "This
is Len. He's like my grandfather. In fact, he's
a grandfather to everyone here on the island. I
would say he would never hurt me, but lately
those words have lost their weight when it comes
to the islanders."

Len grunted, but remorse traced his droopy
eyes. "I'm sad to say it, but I would have to agree.
It pains me to see such upheaval in Berlin."

"Berlin?" Colm repeated.

"You mean Stepping Stones, Len, don't you?"
Gretchen asked.

"Yes, yes, of course." Len looked at the corners of the ceiling. "All because of this house? I don't get it. You have a fine home, Gretchen."

"Well, I appreciate that, Len, but it's going to be a whole lot better when I'm done."

"I don't doubt it, and I don't doubt you. You have to believe that I am on your side." He smiled. "I hope you don't mind I gave myself the tour. Nobody was around when I came in. That attic is impressive, by the way. Are you going to finish it and claim it as your living quarters and let out the rooms on this floor to guests?"

"I would have loved that, but I think I'll make a better income booking the attic. I had hopes it might be an extended rental for the whole summer for someone. I'll make the servants' quarters out back my home."

"You're a wise businesswoman. Always have been, though. The way you helped your mom run the restaurant, it's no wonder Tildy is bent out of shape for losing you. You were more than a waitress and businesswoman, though. You're also a fabulous cook. Your guests will go home ten pounds heavier when they taste your handiwork in the kitchen. I might sell my house and move in." He cackled his oh, so comforting laugh, one that made her want to crawl up into his lap the way she had as a little girl. "Let you take care of me in my last years."

"You're practically a fixture at the Underground Küchen restaurant. Mom would never allow you to leave, too," Gretchen said.

"True enough, especially with the holes in your floor. So many bombs. When will they end?" Len's eyes flitted around the room and his shrunken shoulders folded in. He looked so forlorn that Gretchen reached for his arm.

"Len, is everything okay? You seem confused."

"Is he touched?" Colm whispered into her ear. She shot a questioning look at him. He mouthed back, *Dementia?*

"Of course not," she replied, but the old man's behavior said otherwise. "Len, there are no bombs. I think you're just remembering the war. All is safe here."

Colm grunted. "Your floor's been cut. You call that safe?"

"Cut? What's he talking about? Who cut your floor?" Len snapped back to the present day.

"Everything's fine, Len. Don't worry."

Len eyed them. She was glad to see his keenness restored but wished it weren't focused on her. "Glad to hear it, but you might want to make repairing that hole downstairs a high priority. Wouldn't want you facing a lawsuit so close to your grand opening. Could put a damper on your plans."

"Interesting you should say that." Colm had brought his hammer down but still held it in front of him, tapping the face of the tool into his palm. "Do you have any other tools on you besides that crowbar? A saw, perhaps? One with power, I'd imagine." His threatening stance made Gretchen think he cared about her.

For a split second only.

In actuality, he probably thought the camera was still on him, because the show seemed to be the only thing he cared about.

But he had just helped her through a breathing fit, and there hadn't been any cameras on him then. Unless…

Gretchen's gaze zipped around the room, but quickly she shook her head at her overactive imagination—or a bit of Len's paranoia rubbing off on her. Cameras in the rooms would have to be minuscule pieces of equipment. Spylike even. That settled it. She needed to open for business fast and stop spending her nights watching too many television shows. She zeroed in on Colm's Hollywood-handsome face. Watching too much TV was what gave her a warped sense of reality in the first place. Did she dare believe Colm McCrae's show could really help her get on her feet?

"No saw here," Len responded to Colm's inquiry. "Found this crowbar on the attic stairs."

He passed it over to Gretchen. "Thought the crew out back might need it."

Colm darted to the curtainless window. "My crew's here? They're early."

"Well, I don't know anything about that, but you should have seen that ferry come in this morning all loaded up with machinery and crates and even trailers. That show of yours must be some operation, Mr. McCrae. I've never seen the Sunday ferry make the two-and-a-half-hour boat ride out here for anyone on a Monday."

"Money talks," Colm said as he turned and rushed into the hall. The sound of his boots echoed through the empty house as they hit each step rapidly. The front door slammed.

"Now," Gretchen said, leaning the crowbar against the wall and taking a step closer to Len. "Tell me why you're really here, because it's not for a tour. You could have asked for that before I bought the home. In fact, you've lived on this island since after World War II, so you've probably walked the rooms of this house a million times before it was deserted after Hurricane Bob in '91, and probably after that even. So tell me, Len Smith, what brings you here? More warnings from the islanders? More requests for lengthy dead-end discussions about how I'm ruining the island? How tourists are sure to upset the way of life we've had for generations? I've heard it all. I've listened and taken everyone's feelings into consideration, but no one has done the same for me. Including you."

Len frowned. He walked to the window and leaned his bent frame forward to grip the chipped sill. "I'm old, Gretchen. I don't have much time left."

"Don't say that," she retorted, unable to deny his remark. Especially after she thought how old he looked a moment ago.

He turned toward her, a toothy grin on his cute, wrinkled face. "You want truth? I'm giving you truth. Now listen. You're not too old to bend over my knee, you know." He looked at her with grandfatherly eyes, the love in them sobering her.

She smirked back at him and stepped up to the window. "Whether you all want to believe it or not, I'm not a child anymore. I can make my own decisions now."

Len huffed. "Tell that to your boyfriend."

She felt her lips tighten. "Billy's not my boyfriend anymore. And he never will be again." The television crew down below caught her eye, but her vision was blurred by anger.

"I wouldn't think so with the way he's riling up the town by calling all these meetings to stop you from rehabbing this place. If there was a possibility of a bridge, I'd say he's burned it."

"That has nothing to do with my reason for ending it with him. I needed something he couldn't give me."

"And what was that?"

"Freedom."

Len grunted before saying, "I figured as much."

Gretchen shot a look his way. Did Len know? A geyser of shame doused her. No, he couldn't. There was no way. She averted her gaze back out the window. She caught sight of the director she had met three months ago. He was speaking a little too closely to Colm, although Colm held his ground with folded arms, muscles in forearms flexed. Gretchen wished she could read lips, but by the way Colm's face took on a reddish tinge, it didn't look positive. Was Colm asking Troy about putting her fall through the basement on the cutting-room floor? Or at least what she admitted to after the fall? Gretchen looked back at the director. *What say you, Troy Mullen?*

"No need to pretend with me, Gretchen. I know Billy held on to you a little too tightly. Some would say he meant well."

"Meant well?" She whipped her attention back to the one man she had hoped to have on her side about this. *If* she was ever able to tell. "You have no—"

Len held up a gnarled hand. "I said *some* would say. But still, he's a deputy in the sheriff's department. That holds water. The townspeople like him protecting their island from others with agendas."

"There are no agendas here other than my opening a small bed-and-breakfast to support myself. The crew from *Rescue to Restoration* isn't here for any reason but to help me. When they finish they will be gone forever."

"Are you positive about that?"

"Now you sound like everyone else. Of course, what other reason would there be for them to be here?"

Len shrugged. He leaned in and kissed her forehead. "Just keep your eyes open. Things aren't always what they seem. People aren't always what they seem. Take that TV host for example. I thought he had an Irish accent. When he was in here, I heard no sign of his heritage. What kind of man turns his back on his roots, unless he's got something to hide or gain? I should know. It was over sixty years ago I fled for my life from a Soviet-occupied Germany. I ran with nothing but the clothes on my back and my—"

"I know. Your family's heirloom painting. The painting hung above your family's fireplace for generations and now hangs in my mother's restaurant."

"And will soon hang above your fireplace here."

"What?" Gretchen gasped. "What are you talking about?" Maybe the man was touched, as Colm had put it.

"I've told everyone that I'm leaving you my painting."

"Everyone? Len, the islanders will form a mob against me, my mother in the lead. Why me?"

"Like I said, I'm not getting any younger. It's time I put my ducks in order. As long as my painting hangs, my heritage lives on."

"But my mom would never take it down! You don't have to worry about that."

"I know, but I want you to have it, and that's final."

"That painting has always hung in her restaurant."

"Before the restaurant was your mother's, it was mine. The place represented my new beginning when I came here and opened it for business. If I'm correct this home is your new beginning, right?"

Gretchen nodded, her throat tight with emotion.

"Then I chose well for my legacy to continue." Len looked out the window. "Unlike that television personality down there. What would his father say if he knew his son had let down his family name?"

Gretchen located Colm again below, this time stomping up the steps to a trailer that was placed along the tree line to the woods. Something had made him angry. Had Troy said no to his request on her behalf? Or no to some plan or agenda Colm had on his own? Without knowing who the real Colm McCrae was, she couldn't be certain.

"Maybe you're right," she told Len. "I shouldn't be speaking for people I don't know. I would like to say the crew is only here to help me renovate, but I may be wrong." She reached for Len's hand. "Will you pray for this whole situation? I hate being at odds with the islanders. But I also can't go back to the way things were."

"That bad?" Len squeezed her hand and brought tears to her eyes. She bit the inside of her lip to stop the flow threatening to spill. All she could do was shake her head. If she opened her mouth to speak, only wails of pain and betrayal would come.

"Okay, sweetheart, you don't have to tell me today." Len cupped her cheek so gently it nearly erased the memory of pain there. "But don't wait too long. Nothing can be resolved if you hold it in. Plus, my days are numbered, and I have those ducks I mentioned."

"I said, don't talk like that," she mumbled, wiping away the few spilled tears. "You're going to make me cry again. Plus you're here now, and that's all that matters. Thank you, Len, for being here for me. I really thought the whole island was against me. I don't feel so isolated anymore."

"I'm just sorry you had to feel that way in the first place. So much is changing on my island. And it's not for the better. I just hope I can change the tides back before I take my final breath. Remember what I said, Gretchen—be careful of whom you trust."

"That's easy. From now on, I only trust myself."

"The scene stays?" Colm mumbled in disbelief as he snatched his yellow hard hat from the cabinet inside his trailer. Troy really was mad. Did he want the safety and health administration here shutting them down for unsafe conditions? Ratings were important, but not at the risk of the show—and definitely not at the risk of someone's life, especially the home owner's.

Colm adjusted the strap on the hat with a little more vigor than needed, his thoughts on how Gretchen wanted only to gain her independence from—

He stopped, his argument lingering. From whom? It wasn't as if she was forthcoming with the details. Why should he put his neck on the line for someone so closemouthed? He felt as if he'd spent his whole life helping people who never really wanted his help in the first place. There were only so many hits a guy could take. And yet Colm knew deep down he would take them all, no questions asked. A defender of the underdog he was, through and through.

He resigned himself to asking Troy again to lose the footage, but he knew the only way Troy would consider it was if he got something in return.

Troy had loved that they captured the fall on tape, and he didn't even know about the possibility that someone had cut the boards. Perhaps he should. Then the footage would be considered evidence and they couldn't release it. Nay, that wouldn't work. Knowing Troy he would want it more. And if for some reason he did agree to keep the mishap off the air, who was to say he wouldn't set up another mishap to replace it?

But the director was the least of Colm's concerns. Someone had set out to hurt Gretchen. She could be vulnerable for another "accident" that could leave her dead.

Colm studied the shortened strap length of his hard hat and estimated that it should fit her well now. He'd make sure she wore it 24/7.

He would keep her in his line of vision at all times. And he had to have a talk with his crew right away, tell everyone to be extra careful on the site.

If nothing happened, he could chalk up the floor as a bad accident and move on. In the meantime, the extra security wouldn't hurt anyone, and the view—Gretchen's lovely face—would be right pleasing.

Colm held up the hat and pictured Gretchen's golden curls and petite face peeking out below it, her small jaw jutting in determination. The woman had real *neart istigh*, an inner strength as rare as the near extinct Old Irish Goat. Only prettier.

"What are you smiling about?" The door to the trailer opened wide in front of him, and his newest crew member, Ethan Hunt, crossed the threshold.

"Smiling?" Colm felt his grin drop. "Well, look at that. I guess I was." He put down the hat and brushed it against his thigh. "Glad you're here, though. I was actually heading out to find you."

"Putting me straight to work on my first day, I see." Ethan plunked his duffel bag on the bunk he would be sleeping on for the next three weeks. "What do you need me to do?"

"No orders yet. Besides, it's Troy who hands those out."

"Then why did you want to see me?"

"I'm a little concerned this construction site could contain some unusual hazards. I want the crew to be extra careful. Keep a watch out, especially where the home owner is concerned."

"Ah, now the truth comes out. It's that cute blonde that made you smile." When Colm opened his mouth to negate the idea, Ethan raised his hands. "Hey, I don't blame you. I'd want to protect her, too. She's a real looker."

Colm's stomach churned. Ethan's praise for Gretchen was true, but hearing the man voice such things felt offensive. At one time in Colm's life he would have dropped the hat, then dropped Ethan to the floor. Thankfully for Ethan those fighting days were over.

"Keep things professional, Hunt. We don't need a lawsuit."

"Of course, sorry, I didn't mean anything by it. I guess I'm just excited to be working on the show. It's a real step up from painting real-estate flips. I'm grateful to you for taking me on."

"Your credentials were stellar. Troy and I both agreed right away you would make a great fit.

I said I wouldn't have to babysit you, and Troy said you had a great face for the lady viewers to chat about with their girlfriends."

Ethan laughed. "Glad to hear you really put some thought into it."

Colm smiled in return, letting his ill feeling toward the man slide away. It wasn't as if he hadn't thought the same thing about Gretchen. She was a striking beauty, and Colm was positive every person she met thought it. What did he plan to do—fight every man who found her pretty? He couldn't. He'd made a promise that there'd be no more using his hands for anything but hard work, preferably woodwork.

"I heard about Miss Gretchen's fall earlier today." Concern replaced Ethan's pleasant smile.

"You've heard already?" Colm gripped the hard hat a little tighter.

"Everyone's talking about it. She looked well enough when I saw her walking an old man out to his car, but still, it's disturbing. Are you sure the house is sturdy enough for us to be renovating, or should we demo it instead?"

"It's safe. The construction is old, but it's solid. That's the problem with this whole situation."

"Problem?" Ethan asked with a quizzical expression.

"The house is too sturdy for a break like that to occur unless it was done on purpose."

"Whoa. You think that break was more than old floorboards rotting away?"

A rap on the trailer door saved Colm from speculating further.

"Let's go, Colm," a female voice called through the flimsy steel. "Troy's ready to film you introducing the home owner. Now."

"That's Wendy from makeup. Not a word. Understand? Just keep an eye out around here." Colm headed out the door and allowed Wendy to sponge some stage makeup on him.

"No shiny foreheads allowed," she said in a sweet singsong voice as she gave him a cheeky grin. She looked straight into his eyes when she finished up. "You're the best canvas an artist could ask for. Just handsome." She sighed and stepped back to let him pass.

"You're such a flirt, Wendy. I'm glad I know you're like this with everyone. Do me a favor, though—go easy on the new guy. I need him focused." Then Colm caught Gretchen walking in front of the camera and thought of Ethan's praise of her beauty. "On second thought, have at him," Colm called back to Wendy and walked forward with the hard hat in hand, getting ready to place it on Gretchen's head. He smiled again thinking how adorable she would look in his hat. For the camera, of course. It was only for the camera.

Colm saw Gretchen taking Troy's direction about where to stand. The man had her backing up against a lumber pile. *With all this beautiful scenery?* The ocean was off in the distance on one side, the conifer forest on another. What about the clapboard Victorian they would be working on? So many places would be great backdrops. What was the man thinking?

Gretchen turned, and that was when Colm saw the hazard. A piece of lumber protruded from the pile, level with her head. Troy wanted her to bump her head?

Colm picked up his step, ready to call her to watch out. Only, the next second she reached up and pushed the wood back.

Colm opened his mouth to yell but the spillage of lumber happened so fast that even Gretchen's scream was cut short by the tumbling pieces. All he could see of her as he raced forward was a clump of her corkscrew hair fanned out on the ground around the pile.

"Gretchen," Colm rasped out as he reached her and fell to his knees, not knowing where to start.

"I think it's too late for the hat." Ethan appeared beside him and Colm looked down at the hat still in his hands. "Two mishaps in one day. You just might be onto something, McCrae."

Colm threw the hat aside and dug in. "Help me by clearing some of the wood. Carefully." Colm found a hand and felt for a pulse. "Gretchen, can you hear me?"

Behind him Nate loudly cleared his throat and whispered, "Colm, Irish accent."

Colm ground his teeth at being reminded that he wasn't in charge, but he put his pumping adrenaline into helping Gretchen. "I'm right beside you, Goldie," he assured her with his native accent, but at the same time he thought that no matter how far he distanced himself from Dublin, he still lived and breathed under the weight of a bully.

FOUR

"We really have to stop meeting like this," Gretchen mumbled as she tried to joke for the hovering camera filming her second folly of the day—and with the microphone clipped to her collar, her every word, as well. Playing this off was a must, no matter the pain a load of falling lumber caused.

Colm faced her, the camera behind him unable to capture the wild look of his steely blue eyes. His dilating pupils told her the severity of the situation.

The pain exploding in her head agreed with him.

His face began to blur in front of her, and she dropped her eyelids, needing more time to right herself.

"Someone call 911! She needs a doctor."

"No," she responded, flashing her eyes wide again. Calling the sheriff's office would only dispatch a certain deputy. "I mean, no harm done. I'm fine." Gretchen bit back the pain but was sure she winced when she pushed up. "What's a few sticks of wood?"

Colm scoffed. "About 1.28 pounds per square foot of each two-by-four. You had a good forty boards fall on you. You do the math, *if* you can even think clearly."

"My fault." Gretchen sat straight up and glared, warning him not to make a scene in front of the camera.

He glared right back, but thankfully took her lead.

Gretchen relaxed a bit, ignoring the throbbing. "I don't know what I was thinking pushing that wood back. The pallet had just been transported over on the ferry. It was unstable."

"You shouldn't have been standing here in the first place," Colm said. He looked over her head at Troy standing behind her.

"It's not Troy's fault, either. He didn't tell me to touch the wood. I did that all on my own. But I've learned my lesson for sure. A wood pile is like an apple cart—one wrong move and watch out." She grunted as she pushed up to her feet. "It seems I've been upsetting a lot of apple carts lately. It was only a matter of time before one of them took me down."

Gretchen pushed away Colm's hands that he'd offered to help her up and dusted herself off.

"Kids, don't try this at home." She looked at the camera and hoped her forced smile would belie the true fear she felt.

A few laughs from the solemn crew broke the strained atmosphere. Good, she thought, it was working. *Now if I can just amble out of here to regroup…and maybe cry a little.* But at her first step away from the crowd, Colm shot an arm out to halt her.

"Not so fast," he said.

"I think it's best," she mumbled under her breath.

"Well, I don't." He wasn't looking at her but at the crowd assembled around them, watching intently. About twenty crew members were there to help renovate her home. She had so much to be thankful to them for, but judging by Colm's stare-down he didn't feel the same way. The tension returned thicker than before, and Gretchen didn't need a cue card to know this was not a laughing matter.

Someone had set her up to fall…again.

"Cut." Colm reached over and ripped her mic off her collar. He ripped off his own and threw them to Nate. The man caught them both without a word.

The director yelled, "McCrae, you're over the line. When I am on the set, I say 'Cut.' You do not."

"You had your chance when the wood fell. The fact you kept rolling makes me think you're sadistic. Did you set this up? How about the floor—did you do that, too? You sure arrived a lot earlier than planned. You had ample amount of time."

"Those are dangerous accusations with no basis to back them up, McCrae."

"Increasing your ratings is all the basis you need, and we both know it."

"Perhaps Dumpster-diving should be in your near future again. Or maybe you would rather finish this like old times?" The warning in Troy Mullen's voice set Gretchen backing away from the two men.

Gretchen had no idea what the man meant by his comments. Her head hurt so much now, she really needed to find a place to sit down, preferably away from the grating voices of the men.

She took another step away from Colm. This time he didn't try to stop her. A boulder on the cliff's edge beckoned to her. She could see it through the trees, and she started walking toward the forest. Each step away from the onlookers allowed her to acknowledge the pain radiating through her, but more important, to escape the maliciousness this television show brought to her little island.

Correction: the maliciousness *she* invited.

* * *

Gretchen didn't fool Colm for one second. She walked steadily but so slowly he could tell each step pained her. Why would she try to hide it? Was she like his ma, never admitting to being hurt? Ma always pushed him away, too, just as Gretchen had done when he tried to help her up. But Ma did it out of weakness. There was nothing weak about Gretchen Bauer, so why the refusal to accept help?

"This is going to be a great episode." Troy's voice dragged Colm from his deep thoughts. Colm turned to find a little too much delight on the man's face.

"She could have died," Colm said slowly.

"Oh, it wasn't like it was a pile of bricks that fell on her. Just a few boards. And she looked fine to me. Mighty fine, actually."

Colm's stomach jerked at Troy's meaning. He studied Troy's retreating profile as the man kept his eyes on Gretchen, who was now settling herself down on a large rock on the cliff's edge.

Troy liked her.

That could be dangerous.

When Ethan had praised Gretchen, Colm felt the green prick of envy, but the only sensations rushing through Colm's veins as he watched his boss enter his trailer were fear and concern for Gretchen's safety.

Colm had accused Troy of setting these incidents up for ratings, but what if there was something more between him and Gretchen? What if something happened when Troy had visited the island a few months back to interview her?

Or perhaps didn't happen?

Maybe Troy asked her out and Gretchen told him no. Troy didn't like being told no. But how far would he take his retaliation? Colm had seen the man smear a person's character in public so the person never worked in the industry again.

But Gretchen wasn't in the industry. Troy wouldn't have a way to hurt her other than physically.

Colm looked for the rock she sat on. Her back faced him, but he noticed how she held her head in her hands. Colm fought a growing need to find Troy and make him pay.

"You're not thinking of taking Troy up on that brawl, are you?"

Colm whipped around to find Sly Brewer, the crew's electrician and Colm's friend, approaching.

"How'd you know?"

"The way your fists are all clenched to match your jaw. I thought you might be reverting back to your old ways. You want to share or pray before that happens?"

Colm closed his eyes. Sly was right. "I didn't

start this, but you're right, I might have attempted to finish it. Where would I be without you, Sly? Dead probably. A man can only live so long when he's living by the sword." Colm took a deep breath and let it out slowly.

"Dear Lord, thank You for putting my friend Sly in my life to show me the better way to handle my anger. And as much of a bully as Troy is, I'm thankful for him, too, I guess. Without his giving me this job, I'd still be living on the streets of Dublin, or not living is more like it. And I definitely wouldn't know You, Lord. Not without the wisdom You gave Sly to reach down into the pits to pull me out."

"I'll say amen to that." The balding man smiled. "Now tell me why you think Troy caused that lumber to fall. What's your proof?"

"No proof, other than the dollar signs in his eyes lighting up."

"The man wouldn't put his show at risk, not even for ratings."

"I think it might be something more than ratings motivating him."

"Something like what?"

"Like rejection."

Sly whistled. "We know how Troy doesn't go for any of that when he's on the receiving end."

"Exactly. If you'll pardon me, I need to speak

with the home owner. I'll let you know what she says."

"Sounds good."

"Do me a favor. Keep an eye out on the set for any more of these so-called accidents."

"You can count on me."

"Always. And don't worry about my breaking my promise." Colm walked toward the trees thinking about his old habits. *I won't fall back because of Troy.* There was a better way. There always was.

First, Colm needed to make sure Gretchen was aware she may be in danger. She should probably send the show packing. But she definitely needed to call the sheriff's office and report these incidents so they were on record. She couldn't keep this hidden from the public. It would only leave her more vulnerable and unprotected. What if the next one killed her?

His chest tightened with more worry, but when an image of his mother's face surfaced, he had to ask if this anxiety was more about her. So many years he begged her to file a report. He never understood why she chose to stay under her abuser's control. It made him more determined to keep Gretchen from acting the same way.

And she wouldn't. She'd already proven that, hadn't she? She bought this house to begin her own business, never to depend on another person again, just as she said earlier. She was nothing like his mother. If someone was threatening her new life, she would be the first to stop them.

But what if Colm and his crew were the only way to that new life? Without the show, Gretchen wouldn't have what she was aiming for.

And Troy knows that, Colm thought. The man had the upper hand. Colm had seen it too many times to count.

A movement to his right took his attention away from Gretchen. A blond-haired man stepped out of the tree line and walked toward the young woman. With her back to him, she had no idea he approached. Was he sneaking up on her?

Colm was about to call out a warning, but she must have sensed the guy coming because she half turned his way before Colm could say anything.

She jumped to her feet and took a step back toward the edge of the cliff. A foolish thing to do, but also a telling sign.

This guy wasn't a friend.

Billy. Or, as the islanders referred to him, the handsome, upstanding Deputy Billy Baker.

She knew him differently.

Gretchen could feel the menacing power his

presence had had over her since her senior year of high school. Eight long years she had behaved carefully around him, wondering if his excessive control was in her imagination and wondering what would happen if she tested it. Then one day she tried and found out.

Billy's movements were deliberate and tactful, the sole purpose to invade her space. That was how he worked. He stepped right around the rock without even looking, his eyes locked on his target.

Gretchen lifted her eyes to meet his. They scalded her like lava and caused her foot to involuntarily step back.

Gravel loosened beneath her feet. She'd nearly stepped right off the edge to the roaring ocean below. Her hands reached out on impulse and grabbed his cotton oxford shirt.

He laughed.

Her stomach soured.

She dropped her arms back to her sides and reminded him, "There are people here." Her voice broke, and all she could do was pray silently that someone would hear her if she yelled. If she could even yell. The way her throat tightened, she wasn't sure. "I wouldn't try anything if I were you, Billy. The camera crew arrived today to get set up for the show. They could be filming us right now. You wouldn't want to risk getting caught on camera, would you?"

"Caught doing what? My job? Keeping order is what the town pays me for. That, and protecting the island from the outsiders you've invited here without our approval." Billy leaned in, reminding her that he had her backed to the edge.

One push and she would be washed out to sea. If only the islanders knew they had hired a dictator to patrol their streets. Actually, they did know. That part she'd told them, but it didn't change the fact that their rose-colored ideas for everyone's favorite couple still trumped their good judgment. They shrugged her off as though she acted like a dramatic teenager, confused by a lovebirds' quarrel that would rectify itself when she came to her senses.

Billy reached for her cheek, turning his hand to brush his knuckles against her flesh. A passerby might think it a gentle caress. She knew it was a warning of what the back of his hand felt like on her face, his college ring with its cut stone positioned just right for maximum effect. She didn't need the visual. She remembered daily the last time he'd touched her there, so violently.

She whipped her face away. "Don't touch me," she whispered.

"I worry about you, Gretchen, out here on the

cliffs all by yourself. You should be in town with your mom. With me. You've never been able to make a good decision. Not without my help. You need me, and everyone knows it. They ask me daily if we've made up. You're embarrassing me with this unreasonable quest for self-reliance. That's not what we do here. You've lived on Stepping Stones your whole life. You know that we stand by each other. Protect each other."

"But who will protect me from you?" The words spilled from her mouth before she could stop them. Billy's eyes darkened just as they had six months ago when she'd told him they were through. That was when she'd felt the searing pain to her cheek. How would this encounter end? A shove into the sea?

"That's not fair." He leaned in, eyes beady. "You broke my heart. I've apologized for…losing my cool. You know very well it happened only because I couldn't bear the thought of losing you. We had been together since high school. You promised me forever. Then…this." He jutted his head to the side to refer to the Victorian behind them. "I was losing you to a heap of rotting wood. You can't blame me for being in pain. You caused it. And all I wanted was for you to feel the same way."

Billy reached for her upper arms and his fingers sank deeply into her flesh. One wrong move on either of their parts, and she would lose her footing and fall to her death.

She heard the water crashing over the rocks below. The large, unmovable boulders along Stepping Stones Island were how the island got its name. They'd always made her feel protected and at peace the way they surrounded the island like a shield to the world. Now they were targets for her body to crash against.

"Is everything well, Gretchen?" a familiar Irish brogue asked from behind Billy's towering figure.

Billy turned his head, bringing Colm into her view.

Gretchen exhaled a sigh of relief.

But she wasn't safe yet. One slip was all it would take. Colm must have realized this, too, because he kept his distance. The way his hands fisted at his sides made her realize it was hard for him to stand back.

Billy's fingers squeezed her flesh harder, bringing her attention back to the man who held her life in his hands. How would he react to being caught? Did he care anymore if there were witnesses to his threatening tactics?

"Gretchen, it's not safe for you to be this close to the ledge," Billy said, his voice laced with concern.

Concern she knew to be fake. He liked her on the ledge. It gave him the upper hand.

Billy pulled her against his chest, his hands still clenched to her upper arms. With her face plastered against him she couldn't see his eyes to determine what he planned next. She felt his fingers dig into her again, a clear warning to go along with it. For the moment, she'd have to oblige.

"You're right, Billy," she said. "I shouldn't be out here. I wasn't thinking. My head was hurting me, and I came to sit down."

"What's wrong with your head?"

"It was just a little accident," she answered, not wanting to tell him the whole truth.

He squeezed her arms to remind her of his strength and to demand that she tell him the rest of the story.

"The lumber fell on her," Colm answered for her. She cringed, wanting to shake her head to tell him not to say anything to upset Billy, but that point was moot. Billy had come here upset.

Suddenly, Billy let go of her and spun around to rush Colm, saying, "So she's hurt because of your carelessness? Is that what you're telling me?" Billy's finger jammed into Colm's chest.

Colm barely flinched. "No, she's hurt because someone wanted to cause her pain. You wouldn't happen to know who, would you?"

Billy turned around and reached for Gretchen. She shrank back and Colm said, "The lady has made it clear she doesn't want you touching her." Before she could tell Colm not to bait him, he reached out and grabbed Billy's arm, causing Billy to swing back to lay a punch on Colm's face.

Blood spurted in every direction, but Colm barely responded. He just stood calmly in place.

The lack of response would perturb Billy even more. That was not how he liked his victims. He liked them sniveling on the floor.

"Take your crew and get off my island," Billy demanded.

"It's not just your island, and we were invited here to help Gretchen start a new life. If the islanders cared about her, they would see she's worked hard for this and would support her."

Billy brought back his arm to throw another punch. Gretchen started to shout to Colm to watch out. She didn't get the first syllable out before Colm had Billy's arm twisted up behind him and the deputy bent over the rock.

It happened so fast. She'd never seen anything like it.

"I'll not be brawlin' with you," Colm said with his Irish accent deeper than ever. "But I'll also not be takin' any more of your deckin'." He sounded dangerous, as though he would explode in any minute. She stepped back from the scene, unsure who scared her more. The vise grip Colm had on Billy left her ex helpless and weakening by the second. Billy's brute strength had nothing on Colm's.

Billy grunted and whimpered. He could really be hurt if this went on. Gretchen knew she shouldn't care, but it wouldn't solve anything. Billy was a law-enforcement officer, even if he was out of uniform. Colm would be in a lot of trouble.

"Colm," she said, "let him go. The town's just a little on edge lately. I can handle it."

Colm cast her an angry glance. "He had his hands on you. If that's how your town treats you, maybe you should get a new town."

"I'll manage it on my own."

"Right." Colm released Billy with a shove and stepped back. Blood covered Colm's face. He acted as though it wasn't the first time he'd been hit. "I'll let you deal with it your way, but if I see another person touch you like that again, I don't care who they are, I'll step in again."

Billy got up off his knees and faced Colm. This time, he kept a distance. The look in his eyes, though, showed no fear. "You'll regret it if you do. This isn't over."

Billy stepped toward the trees but stopped before he reached them. "Send them away,

Gretchen, if you know what's good for you." He sent a scathing look toward Colm and turned to disappear into the conifers.

Silence fell between her and Colm. Neither said a word, and he still had yet to wipe away the blood. At least it seemed the flowing had stopped. "Doesn't that hurt?" she asked, nodding to his face.

"I'm sorry," he replied, totally not answering her question. His shoulders slumped and for the first time, he looked as if he was about to fall to his knees. But not from pain. "I'm so sorry for losing it like that."

"Losing it? He punched you. You were just defending yourself. And doesn't that hurt?" she asked again, stepping close, her hand nearly touching his face.

"You don't understand. I made a promise. After my da died, my ma remarried a man who lived by his fists and taught me to be just like him. But God rescued me from that violence, and I promised Him I would never be like Gil Griffin again."

"Hey, you're not," Gretchen said soothingly, even though she wasn't so sure after what she had just witnessed. She reached for his hand, but it was as if she wasn't there. She could never convince him of his innocence, not when he believed he'd broken a promise to God. All she could do was help him. She looked toward the house and the crew working about. She saw the trailers in the opposite direction. "Do you have any ice in your trailer?"

He nodded, but his conflicted eyes didn't register why she asked.

"Let's go. I'll get you cleaned up. Your nose looks like it might be broken, but I can at least get rid of the blood."

Colm let her lead the way. "You don't have to do this. I know how to clean up my own messes."

"I take that to mean you've been in this situation before."

"Too many times to count."

Gretchen didn't turn to face him. Walking in front of him allowed her to be free with her questions, and hopefully, he would be unguarded with his answers.

"Where did you learn to fight like that? I mean the way you took Billy down was professional."

"It was dirty. Plan and simple. It's the way I learned to fight."

"Where?"

"In my old life. On the streets of Dublin, love."

Gretchen stopped and searched his face. His words could have sounded romantic with his thick accent, but instead she felt as though he had opened an old wound in front of her. It took all her strength not to ask if the dirty street fighter was the real Colm McCrae. She had yet to get a good read on him, but so far the two sides of Colm she'd witnessed didn't gel at all.

"Billy Baker is a deputy in the sheriff's department," Gretchen said while she removed ice from Colm's small freezer. She filled a plastic bag, jiggling the cubes as she came to where he leaned against the small dinette table. "After that altercation you can probably expect a visit from Sheriff Owen Matthews."

"I hope the man does pay me a visit," Colm answered. "I'd love to tell him how his deputy manhandled you. I would think an officer of the law would know better. Wouldn't you?"

Gretchen held the ice in front of him. She froze as solid as the water. Her eyes flitted side to side before landing on the bag between them.

"Well, wouldn't you? The man had no right to touch you. I don't care if the town is up in arms about your opening a B&B. You should press charges, Gretchen. Don't let him get away with this."

She lifted her sea-blue eyes to his. "No harm done," she said abruptly as she brought the ice to his swelling face. A hissing sound escaped his throat at the contact. "Except for you, I suppose. For someone who obviously knows how to fight, I'd think you would know how to duck, as well."

"You're changing the subject."

"Yes, I am. Now let it go."

Colm studied the twitch in her cheek and the guarded look in her eyes. She seemed to be focused on his injury, but he knew the tactic was a cover-up. She closed him out even as she gently took care of him. It would appear the hospitable bed-and-breakfast owner-to-be had hung a shingle over her heart that said No Vacancy.

"This wouldn't be the first time I've stood alone in protecting a woman from a bully. I'm not afraid."

"This, coming from the man who got a busted-up nose for sticking it where it doesn't belong. Perhaps you might want to rethink this fearlessness."

"Never. I'll take the banjaxed nose any day over allowing some brute to take his anger out on an innocent woman."

"Who said I was innocent?"

Colm spoke from behind the ice bag, "Trust me. No man has a right to put his hands on you, no matter what you think you deserve."

"So, how did you go from the streets of Dublin to Hollywood?"

Another attempt to change the topic. He gave in.

"I was actually interfering in another incident where a young woman was being accosted. One day I was eating out of garbage cans with my bare hands, the next Troy was handing me caviar on fine china. All because I stood up against an injustice."

"I don't understand. How did that happen? Who was the girl? Someone famous?"

"No, she was a waitress in a pub. Troy's crew was filming in Dublin and a few stopped off for a drink. One of them said something off-color to the waitress. I didn't like it and I said so. Few hours later, he faced me in the alley outside. Not a good move on his part. I really roughed him up, and just as I knocked him out, an officer showed up to arrest me. We were on a first-name basis, the cops and I, so it was my word against the other guy's. Let's just say my word didn't count for much."

Her eyes grew skeptical. "But how did a back-alley brawl bring you to fame and fortune?"

"One word—Troy. He appeared out of the shadows and fixed everything. The next thing I knew, the officer was gone with a payoff from Troy, the crew member was chopped, and I was offered the job of a lifetime. When Troy told me it was a show about renovating old houses, I couldn't believe it. I jumped at the offer. My da was a carpenter, and now I could get off the streets and follow in his footsteps instead of my stepfather's. Or at least I thought I could. Troy doesn't care that I would rather be working on the houses than hosting the shows. He just tells me to smile for the camera. Oh, and talk the way I do. Can't forget that."

Gretchen tilted her head. Colm bit back an appreciative smile. She really was pretty as a picture. "Your accent. Why do you not want to use it?"

"It's a sure sign of my roots. Even in Dublin I grew up being bullied for my accent. I worked real hard to lose it, tame it so I would sound more posh, as they say. More D4."

"D4?"

Colm laughed at how silly it sounded. It wasn't so long ago when it had been all that mattered. "The D4 accent is how the middle class speak in South Dublin. Named for the D4 postcode. But even that wasn't enough. I wanted to wipe my tongue clean of anything Irish and listened to a lot of BBC pronunciation to help me along."

She pulled the ice from his face to look at him. "What's wrong with being Irish?"

"Nothing. It just reminds me of things I want to forget."

"Like what?"

"Things I want to forget."

"Right, got it." Gretchen smiled, her lips curved in such a lovely way he nearly reached up to touch them. Her free hand reached toward him and he thought she was of the same mind. She wouldn't hear him complaining.

Suddenly a searing pain shot through him, shocking the air right out of him. He might have howled in pain but wasn't sure because of the screaming agony zipping through his face straight to the back of his head.

She hadn't been reaching for his lips, but for his nose.

"Oh, I'm so, so sorry," she said. "I thought I could push it back in place if I did it fast enough."

Colm breathed and grunted through the pain. "It's grand. I can handle it. Really. Just grand." He forced a smile.

She shook her head with a smirk. "Sure it is, Mr. Tough Guy. And how will you handle your boss when he sees your nose?" She covered his face with the ice again.

"He'll probably threaten to fire me. He does that a lot. But I don't think he will. I'm his bread and butter. I'll have to compensate him in some way, though."

"Why's that?"

"Simple. I owe him. And he reminds me of this daily."

Colm took the bag of ice from her bright pink hand. He reached for her and felt how cold the fingers were from holding the ice for so long. He held on tight and squeezed, willing his warmth to seep in.

"Gretchen, while we're talking about Troy, I noticed when the lumber fell on you, he smiled. It could be his twisted sense of humor, but I also couldn't help but wonder if the two of you had a past together. Perhaps when he came to the island to interview you. Had the two of you dated?"

Gretchen inhaled sharply. She ripped her hand from his grasp and said adamantly, "I will never date another man ever again. Ever."

"'Again'? Bad experience in college?"

"I never went to college. In fact, I've barely left the island for more than a quick visit to the mainland. My boyfriend never wanted me to stray too far."

"Boyfriend? Sounds a little overprotective— wait. The deputy. That brute is your boyfriend?"

"He *was* my boyfriend. Not anymore."

"Are you sure he knows that? From what I

could see he hasn't accepted your dismissal."
Rampant thoughts crowded Colm's head. "You
know what this means, don't you? Your deputy
has motive. He could be the one who cut your
floor, and not because you want to open a B&B,
but because you dared to go against him."

Gretchen's eyes drifted closed, but no argument formed on her lips.

"I can see this idea doesn't surprise you.
Something you've already thought through?"

A knock sounded on the metal door. "Colm,
daylight wanes," Sly called. "Troy wants you
out here. We still have hours of filming tonight."

Gretchen turned, taking the opportunity to
beat a fast retreat.

"Not so fast!" Colm stopped her with his
commanding words. "Deputy Baker is the man
who hurt you before, isn't he?"

Her small shoulders rose and fell, but no denials came his way.

A sudden burst of anger roared through him,
so familiar he knew it would always be a part of
him. He would never escape it. No matter how
far he ran from those slummy streets of Dublin, from the heavy fists of his stepfather, this
feeling of having no control over this heated response would stay with him forever.

*Father God, help me to control my need to
take matters into my own hands.* Colm clenched

his fists but kept immobile, not trusting what he would do if he went after the guy; he knew the deputy would surely pay the price for Colm's backslide. This small woman standing in front of him had felt the strength of Baker's hands. So why shouldn't the lawman feel Colm's? The rationale whirled through his mind with not a single counterargument to sway him to stay.

Except his promise to God.

Colm relaxed. "Did you contact the sheriff when Baker hurt you?" he asked quietly.

No answer. Now her no-vacancy sign blared bright neon pink. She wasn't going to share anything with him. But that wouldn't stop him from protecting her any way he could.

Colm reached for another one of his hard hats. Adjusting the strap, he walked up behind her and gently placed it on her head of soft curls. His fingers brushed up against her hair, memorizing the feel of its texture. One curl looped around his index finger before he reluctantly let it spring away.

"You don't have to talk about it, but you do need to wear my hat. For your own protection, and for my sanity. I'm going to do my best to make sure nothing else happens to you."

She swirled slowly around, her eyes glittering with unshed tears. But it wasn't the tears that moved him. It was her look of doubt warring with her need to believe him that nearly caused Colm to reach out for her again.

"How do I know you're not just like him?"

Colm kept his hands at his side, but knew they rested in their natural fisted pose. "The sad truth is, Goldie, I am just like him."

FIVE

"Quiet on the set." Troy quelled the room with his booming direction. "Wendy, you're not painting a masterpiece. Colm's got enough makeup on. Move it." After Wendy's grumbling departure, Troy gave a nod to Colm and said, "Action."

"Welcome back to day three at The Morning Glory B&B, and boy, do I have some grand news for you." Colm smiled at the camera. It came easily for him because he liked the person the camera saw. If only everyone's favorite TV carpenter was more than just a role to play.

"I mentioned yesterday the home owner had a surprise for us, and I have just been informed what it is. It would appear Gretchen is not only a beauty but handy around the house. A real jack-of-all-trades, she is. Today she will demonstrate her skills by installing a hot tub in one of the guest suites. I have to admit, I have my doubts." He put his finger to his lips and made a shushing sound at the camera.

Gretchen, who stood by the tub with a pair of joint pliers in hand, did not look amused at his antics.

But she did look adorable.

From beneath her hard hat she rolled her eyes to the gutted ceiling of the bathroom. All the old tiled walls were already removed, exposing the wiring and copper plumbing that she would now connect to the tub.

"Oh, Mr. McCrae," she said in a sweet mimic of his accent. "You're just jealous because you don't get to play with the tools. That's why you're only the host."

"Whoa! And the gloves come off!" Colm shot back. "What do you say we take this out back? Huh, Goldie?"

"Sorry, no can do. Some of us have to earn a living by doing real work. Perhaps you can go practice your smile in a mirror while the rest of us make some progress on the house."

Gretchen's pursed lips twitched. She was holding back a smile he hoped she would let fly, even if it was at his expense. Her face was meant for television. He'd seen some of the footage already, and the camera loved her. But then it was quite easy to do, especially with her glittering eyes beneath the hard hat stealing the spotlight.

When Colm had envisioned her in his hat, he had expected her to look fetching in it, but he hadn't expected the pummeling his gut took every time she looked his way. No alley brawl had ever bowled him over as much. He could gaze upon her for a lifetime and never tire of it.

Colm choked out a laugh, nearly forgetting the camera rolled. He must look like a lovesick puppy with his tongue hanging out. *Get back into character*, he scolded himself. The crew stood by waiting for him to respond.

"Shall we cue the cricket sounds, Mr. Mc-Crae?" Gretchen asked, then faced the camera. "It would appear our smooth-talking Irish host is speechless."

Colm cleared his throat at the large round lens. Tongue-tied was more like it, he thought. "Yes, well, I do believe Round One goes to you, Goldie, because I've got nothing. All right, love, impress us with your plumbing capabilities, and I suppose I'll just slink away to find that mirror you mentioned for a little more practice."

"Don't you go anywhere. You could use the lesson just like your viewers. Probably more so." She smiled and winked at him, but quickly became all business.

Gretchen turned to point out the two parallel pipes running down into the floor, and reaching out with the pliers, she touched metal against metal with a tinking sound. "These pipes are old, but they're in great shape. To cut costs, I decided to keep whatever fixtures I could. The fittings will match up to the new tub just fine. The electrical wiring has already been connected to the tub, thanks to Sly." She grinned at the show's electrician, who also stood in the shot.

Colm noticed a pink tinge race up Sly's leathery neck. It would appear her smile affected his friend, too.

"Since I know a bit about plumbing," she continued, "I wanted to do the honors of connecting the pipes and turning on this hot tub for the first time. I was so excited when the director suggested it, so thanks goes to Troy for this opportunity."

"Gretchen, can you tell us a wee bit about where you learned these tools of the trade?" Colm asked.

She hesitated, her cheeks red. After too long a pause she said, "Sure, I suppose I could." The footage would have to be edited, but Colm wondered why she had a hard time sharing anything about her life. Her secrets ran deep, whatever they were.

She sat on the edge of the tub and faced the camera. "After my dad passed away when I was seven, I used to try to show my mom we were okay on our own. I learned everything I could to help around the house. Even fixing a leaky pipe. Some days I feel like I'm still trying to prove it to her, you know? I keep thinking that maybe after this show she'll finally see there's nothing wrong with being on your own, and in fact, we can be stronger because of it." Gretchen gave a short laugh, but it fell flat, as did her smile. "Anyway, I tried it her way once…um… dating, I mean…" Gretchen visibly gulped and blanched at the camera.

Colm couldn't let her bomb on film, especially since he'd set her up by asking the question. "So, you set out to better your family's life. I commend you. It couldn't have been easy, but here you are, proof that it can be done. You're an inspiration to us all, Goldie." Colm turned his head enough to shield half his face from the camera. He hoped his supportive gaze encouraged her to continue.

"Well, thank you, Colm. And I'm sorry for what I said about you and the tools." Her smile grew broader by the second, and his respect for her grew, as well. Her blue eyes shimmered with life again. "But not about the mirror." She stood and turned her back to him.

Colm looked back at the camera, eyes wide. "Aaaand Round Two also goes to Goldie."

"Score! So, let me show how to install a tub. It's really quite simple. As you can see, we've already mortared the tub into place beneath this beautiful picture window looking out to the rocky sea coast. Could you think of a better view while you relax in a hot tub? The guests who request the Sea View room will be in for a treat. Which reminds me, I'm already accepting reservations and my planner is filling up for the summer season, so don't wait to call. Anyway, now the tub is ready to be hooked up to these parallel pipes called the waste, overflow and trap pipes." She waved her pliers at each pipe as she named it, then started with the waste pipe.

She reached out to grab the pipe, but just as the tips of her fingers brushed against it, a spark zapped her and sent her flying back and onto the floor with a thud.

Gasps circled through the room.

Gretchen had dropped the pliers and lay against the tub. She held her injured hand close to her body, shaking.

"Gretchen?" Colm dropped to his knees, grabbing her hand. "Let me see," he demanded, noticing two of her fingertips blackening. He looked at her pained expression, her eyes tightly sealed. "Goldie, look at me." He reached for her face with his free hand, patting her cheek to get her attention. He needed to know if she could comprehend what had happened. Her eyes opened but looked so stunned, he didn't think she did.

"This doesn't make sense," she murmured.

"Being shocked while installing a tub, you mean?"

She nodded. "That's not supposed to happen." She lifted her blackened fingers. "How?"

"Sly will figure it out." Colm noticed his friend already inspecting the pipes. "Right now I need to know if you're okay."

"I think so. Just stunned and really confused. Sly, wh-what happened?"

Colm dragged his gaze away from searching for any injuries on Gretchen to look at the electrician. "Does this have anything to do with an old house not being grounded? Is it as simple as that? Please let it be as simple as that," Colm said under his breath as he pulled Gretchen's shaking body closer to his, butting his head against her hard hat. A lot of good it had done her. He ripped it off and tucked her head into his neck.

Sly ripped a voltage reader from his belt and touched it to the pipe. "There's electricity looking for a ground, all right. And it'll take anything it can get, including a human body. The waste pipe is hot."

"Hot?" Colm felt inadequate. What did a woodworker and reality television show host know about electricity? "Come on, Sly. You know when it comes to electricity I'm as handy as an ashtray on a motorbike. What does 'hot' mean?"

"As in hot-wired. Come here. I'll show you."

Colm wasn't ready to relinquish Gretchen from his hold, but her need to see what had happened trumped his. She pulled herself out of his arms to crawl over to Sly.

"It would appear someone attached the positive side of a hot wire to the copper piping. They used the hot tub's electrical box for juice. Nicely done, I might add. Very clean and discreet. I wouldn't have noticed anything out of place if I hadn't been looking for it. Man, if she had grabbed hold of the pipe with her whole hand…well, let's just say things would have been a whole lot worse than burned fingers."

Colm swallowed the bile rising in his throat. Facts first. Then reaction. "But you just hooked up all the electricity last night." He looked from the tampered pipe to Sly.

"Which means someone came in after I left."

"How do I know it wasn't you?" Colm choked on the words even before he finished saying them. "I'm sorry, Sly. I'm not thinking clearly. Of course you would never do anything like this. Forgive me."

"Nothing to forgive, son. This is serious business and you've got foul play to contend with. At this point, it could be any one of us."

Gretchen scanned the faces in the room. "Who else was with you when you worked on the electricity?" she asked Sly.

"This is a television show. There's always someone around. Colm was even here while we filmed."

Gretchen shot a look Colm's way. He saw her reservations about him once again flowing into her eyes. He put a hand on her shoulder and could feel her doubts in him tense up her body.

"Cut," Troy announced. "That was perfect. Sorry, Gretchen, about you being hurt. Glad it was just a minor shock. It wasn't planned, but you definitely played it well. Got some great footage to work with. Love that look of fear you gave Colm."

Gretchen pushed Colm away and jumped to her feet. "I wish I never called this show. I think you should all leave."

"Terms, Miss Bauer." Nate peeked out from behind his camera.

Wendy chimed in, "Stuff like this is why the home owners aren't on the scene during reno- vation and shooting. For your safety you might want to reconsider, Gretchen."

Gretchen's mouth dropped. "You make it sound like this was my fault. Someone did this to me!" She raced out of the room and down the stairs. Her front door slammed and rattled the windows around them.

After a few beats of guilt-filled silence, Colm said, "I'm heading out to shut the power down. Sly, don't touch the pipe. I want Gretchen to report this to the authorities first. Someone knew she would be working up here today. Someone planned for her to grab hold of that pipe and not let go. Not even after she fried."

Gretchen ran toward the trees and her cliff. She had to get away to think.

"Gretchen, wait up!" Colm called from behind her and she picked up her speed.

She gave no answer, just darted looks in all directions. The incident had freaked her out to the point that she had asked the crew to go. What was wrong with her? Even if she hadn't signed the contract, she needed them. Without them she would never make her deadline.

"You have to call the sheriff, Gretchen." Colm grabbed her hand to make her stop and look at him. "Listen to me. Your life is more important than any business."

"You don't understand. You're rich. You can buy any home you want. Start your life anywhere you want."

"First of all, Troy pays me the bare minimum and the money I do make, I put aside for—

Never mind. This conversation is not about my finances. It's about your life…and whatever you think you need to prove to someone, like you mentioned inside. Is this why you won't call the sheriff's department? Or are you still trying to protect a certain deputy?"

"How dare you throw that at me!" Gretchen yanked her hand away. "I shouldn't have told you anything!"

"You can trust me, Gretchen. I'm not throwing it in your face. I just don't want you to protect the man who hurt you. It will never end if you do."

"Is this about your ma and the man she remarried? Because I'm not her."

"No." Colm reached for her arms. "This is about you. Gretchen, you could have been killed. If you had grabbed hold of the pipe, you wouldn't have been able to let go. And nobody would have been able to help you. Not even me. I'm doing my best to protect you, but someone wants to make sure that task is impossible. Please, if you won't call for yourself, who will you call for? Your mom?"

Tears threatened to spill from her eyes, but not from anger. Betrayal hurt so much more. "My mom would be on his side. She has been since the day we became a couple. Even when I ended it."

"Oh." Colm pulled her into his chest. He wrapped his arms tight and spoke into her ear. "I'm so sorry, love. The one person you should be able to go to—"

"A little lovebird quarrel?" A rude voice intruded abruptly. A quick twist and she saw Troy approaching. His gaze traveled between them for the answer.

"Of course not," she jumped to reply first, then extricated herself from Colm's arms.

Troy grunted, obviously doubting her claim. "Too bad. I could have used that."

Colm tilted his head. "You know, Troy, Gretchen might have been killed. You don't seem too upset about that fact."

Troy scoped her out from top to bottom then back again with a shrug. "I said I was sorry. What more do you want?"

"I want to know who besides you knew Gretchen would be installing the tub today."

"I had nothing to do with this incident, if that's what you're insinuating."

"Then tell me who else knew! Because if you're the only one, you're going to need a lawyer. I'm not going to sit back and allow you to put people in harm's way for an inconsequential show on the telly."

Troy huffed. He unbuttoned the dark green suit that looked tailor-made and closed in on

Colm. "Inconsequential show? Need I remind you of the Dublin prison you would call home if it wasn't for that show? Now, I don't know anything about a hot wire. And I can't say for certain who else knew about the installation. But if you want to call it quits and head back to your filthy neighborhood, go right ahead."

"No." Gretchen intervened before she lost her one chance at making a go of her business. "As much as I want to send you all packing right now, I can't. I…I…"

"You what?" Colm demanded. "You *need* us? Is that what you were going to say? It's not that hard, you know. Go ahead, try it. 'I need you.' Say it."

"You know I do. I hate it more than anything, but I need you to start this business. I need you to help me begin my life again. There, you happy?"

"I won't be happy until you call the sheriff's department and report these incidents."

"Then you might as well start swimming for the mainland now, because if I let the islanders know what's going on, they will use it to put a stop to the renovation and the opening of The Morning Glory. Don't you see?"

"The only thing I see is a woman with a lot of enemies who needs a bodyguard, not a construction crew. What *I* would hate more than anything is to see you get killed." Colm's jaw trembled with pent-up anger. He stomped away, clenching and unclenching his fists. He stopped suddenly and turned back, and Gretchen caught a glimpse of the street-fighting Colm.

Her heart jumped into her throat, but just as fast as it came, his anger turned to sadness and his shoulders slumped. He let out a sigh. "Just call the sheriff, Gretchen. Please."

The pleading look he gave her nearly made her nod. She had to avert her attention away from his face.

"Then at least watch where you walk and what you touch. This place is a ticking time bomb. I need to go shut the power off for Sly."

She watched in silence as Colm walked to the back of the house where the exterior entrance to the basement was located.

"You don't fool me," Troy said from behind her. She had nearly forgotten he stood there, witnessing her and Colm's confrontation.

"What are you talking about?"

He pressed close with two steps of his long legs. "You just told me there was nothing between you and McCrae. Three months ago, when I asked you out you also told me you would not be involved with another man for the rest of your life. Your words don't speak as loud as your actions." He leaned down so their faces were inches apart. His eyes turned beady and severe. She studied them with growing concern for her safety.

This is what danger looks like.

"I know there's something between the two of you." Troy spoke low and evenly. "I've watched the footage when the two of you are on camera together. The chemistry is off the charts. But there's something you should know about Colm and his type of chemistry—things tend to blow up around him."

"Like the fight you ransomed him from for your gain?"

Troy laughed but kept his voice quiet. "You mean when I saved him from a jail cell?"

"He was attacked."

"So he says." Troy straightened. He dusted off the lapel of his fancy suit. "You know, I think I'm going to let this little fling continue. If nothing else, I'll make a pretty penny off this episode. People who don't even care about home renovating will keep the channel tuned in just to see what happens between the two of you. Do me a favor, though—save these quarrels for the camera. The viewers will eat them up." He flashed his too-white teeth and stepped toward the house.

Gretchen's hand went to her chest where she could feel it tightening. The events of the day and Troy's demeanor were doing a number on her breathing. She looked to her bedroom window and wondered if she had an old inhaler upstairs in her medicine chest.

"Oh, and, Gretchen," Troy called out. He continued to walk on as though he knew she still stood by. "Just so you know, my offer stands. When you're done slumming with McCrae, you know where to find me. Especially since I now know you haven't really sworn off men. You just like the heavy hitters." He disappeared around the back of the house, and she heard the first wheeze in her chest.

Colm stepped down the hatchway stairs. At the landing he pulled the bulb string overhead to light his way and noticed the metal casing straight across on the far wall. The electrical panel showed Gretchen had done a fine job updating the fuses to breakers. The woman really was quite talented to be able to handle these tasks on her own. It was too bad she never went to college. Or, more appropriately, wasn't allowed to go to college.

"I've seen the hold a person can have over another. Even a smart one such as yourself, Gretchen. But if I do nothing else for you here, I will do my best to show you you never deserved that kind of treatment. I promise," he vowed aloud and flipped the breaker. The basement went dark…but not silent.

A thudding noise came from his right. The sunlight streamed down the stairs but the rest of the basement remained in the shadows and gave no clues to what caused the noise. He listened for more but heard nothing.

A scraping sound from behind made him whip around, but before he could move three inches, pain exploded in his head. His knees gave out beneath him and the cold dirt floor abruptly met his cheek. Colm bounced twice as a different kind of darkness seeped into his mind.

Gretchen. He said her name again and again but wasn't positive his lips actually formed any sound. If they were anything like his useless limbs, he only thought her name.

But he had to move. Without his protection, she would be in more danger now than ever. He had to get to her, but his body wouldn't budge. A black swirl hovered over him. The desire to let it take him over strengthened, but he clenched his jaw and lifted his head enough to see a blurred movement on the hatchway stairs. A flash of the color green mixed with the blackness threatening to overtake him. He had to let it, and his cheek met dirt again.

Was the person wearing green? Was that

where the color came from? Colm forced his throbbing head back up and squinted to look again, but suddenly the doors closed, shutting out all light.

And all hope of him keeping any of the promises he made to Gretchen.

SIX

Gretchen wheezed a bit as she skirted the orange construction cone covering the hole in her floor. She took a step up her railing-less foyer staircase, hoping her old spare inhaler awaited her upstairs, and hoping she wouldn't meet another mishap along the way.

Was a business really more important than her life? Colm had asked.

Her answer was no, of course, but the lack of a staircase railing was only a small example of all the work that needed to be completed before she could open for business. Without the crew, she'd never see her grand opening.

Her foot landed gently on the next tread without a bomb going off. Colm's other words alternated with his question: *Please watch where you walk and what you touch.* He had her second-guessing her every move.

Check that.

Whoever was setting up these guerilla traps

had her second-guessing her every move. Even washing her hands would come with the question: *Am I going to die when I turn on this faucet?*

Her feet hit the top step with no outright ambushes. She inhaled without a wheeze and took that as a good sign. Still, she wanted her inhaler with her, even if only a few puffs were left on it. It was better than nothing if this subtle asthma issue became a full attack.

In the bathroom, the sight of her pale complexion in the medicine cabinet's mirror pulled her up short. She looked defeated.

But by whom?

Billy?

Troy?

Her mother? Gretchen scoffed at the idea but really couldn't put it past the great and powerful Tildy Bauer. The woman practically ran the town. What had Gretchen been thinking when she thought she could break out from under Tildy's controlling thumb? It cut her deep that she even had to. Her own mother had chosen Billy's side over her daughter's. Tildy never believed in her, not even when she was a child. Gretchen's chest tightened and she pulled the door wide to find the inhaler. The counter dial on it said it had one dose left. She closed the door and held it to her lips but didn't press down to release the medicine.

She studied her face and eyes. Her white face may have said the fight was over, but the eyes said not yet.

But who was her adversary?

An image of Colm and his clenched fists popped into her head.

She quickly dismissed it. It couldn't be Colm. He abhorred men mistreating women. The last time he had witnessed a woman being insulted, he was nearly thrown in jail for defending her.

But he hadn't been.

Instead he got the job of a lifetime.

Seemed to have benefited him well.

So what? She couldn't fault the guy for receiving a blessing from God. She dismissed the direction her mind took with Colm. He was on her side. Thanks to him she wasn't alone in this fight.

Gretchen removed the inhaler and pocketed it. The idea of having someone on her side gave her all the lift she needed.

The idea that it was Colm had the color rushing back to her cheeks.

In addition to her flushed cheeks, though, guilt reflected back at her. "He's only a friend," she said aloud, but didn't miss the way her lips frowned at her claim.

Before she talked herself into easing up on her vow of independence, she headed to the Sea View room's bath, where the pipe incident had occurred. No one was around now but Gretchen could see the hot wire had been removed. She flicked the lights, but nothing happened. Why hadn't Colm turned the power back on? As she turned to walk out, she noticed his bucket of tools tipped over and its contents spilled.

She also noticed his tools were shiny and new.

She laughed. During filming, she had been joking, but Troy really didn't let Colm use the tools.

Typically, he carried his bucket with him, but could it be all an act? What had he said in his typical Dublin lingo? *I'm as handy as an ashtray on a motorbike.*

Was that the truth? Was Colm McCrae nothing but a face on TV? The idea clutched at her heart. There had to be more to him than looks and a smooth voice.

Please, God, don't let him be another smooth-talker. I don't think my judgment of character could take another hit.

Gretchen knelt to right the bucket. She tossed a few wrenches and screwdrivers back into it, then picked up his jigsaw cutter. She dropped it and went after a tape measure lying a foot away. She placed that inside as well, but just as she stood, she noticed the jigsaw had overturned with its blade up. Except it wasn't up. On further inspection, she saw it was bent.

Why would Colm have a bent jigsaw blade? He must have used the saw for something too thick. Something like...

Gretchen paused and craned her neck toward the stairs.

Something like her wooden floorboards?

Was the bent blade proof that Colm was behind cutting her floor? She didn't want to believe it but he had been on the property when she returned home that first day. Could it have been him all along?

A pain of betrayal zinged her worse than the voltage had. She may have questioned Colm's involvement when she first met him, but deep down, she didn't believe him to be the source.

How could she not, now?

But why would he do such a thing?

Maybe setting up these mishaps was his way of breaking away from Troy to start out on his own, so he'd make all the money. All Colm had to do was stage a few accidents, come running into the fray to rescue her like a knight in shining armor—or the handsome host in stage makeup in his case. Get the viewers to love him and his chivalrous ways, and just as Troy had said, the viewers would eat it up.

But would Colm really have tried to electrocute her on film? Maybe he would have pulled her out of the way before she grabbed hold of the electrified pipe.

Maybe not.

Gretchen wheezed but refrained from reaching for the inhaler. She'd need the last puff for backup.

Because she wasn't giving up yet.

From now on, though, she would keep a watchful eye on every person, including Colm. She also wouldn't share what she planned to work on with anyone beforehand. There would be no time for someone to sabotage her efforts the way he or she had with the pipe.

With her plan set, Gretchen reached for the jigsaw and headed downstairs. She had to see his face when she showed it to him. She hoped he had nothing to do with it, but if he did, she hoped he wouldn't deny it. She didn't think she could take another's lies.

Gretchen burst out her front door and hurried around the house. The trailers were off in the distance, and she picked up her steps through the grass.

"Help!" A call from above pulled her up short.

She gave a quick look to see Ethan standing on top of a ladder, holding on to the shutters to one of the upstairs windows, his knuckles white.

"Is everything all right?" Gretchen walked over, peering up at the painter, who looked as though he'd never stepped foot on a ladder before. *A renovation TV host who doesn't know what blade to use when cutting wood. A painter who doesn't know how to use a ladder.*

Ludicrous didn't come close to describing these scenarios. What kind of crew had she invited?

"Am I glad to see you. Everyone's at lunch, and I need someone to hold the ladder so it doesn't tip back. Would you mind?"

Gretchen controlled the face she wanted to make. "Sure, no problem," she said and tossed the jigsaw down onto the grass so she could brace the ladder with both hands. "Come on down."

As soon as Ethan let go of the shutter, it swung out. He must have broken it away from the house when he reached out to steady himself before.

This eye roll she let go.

A moment later, pain sprang to her neck. "Ow!" She let go of the ladder to reach for her neck. Then pain struck her arm. A third occurred on the other side of her neck. Buzzing erupted on her left side.

Bees. Bees were all around her!

Gretchen looked up to see a swarm chasing

Ethan down the ladder and backed away as two more stung her. "Ethan! Hurry up!" she yelled, swatting more away from her face.

"Go, Gretchen! Run around to the back of the house. Get away from here!" Ethan jumped from the eighth rung and landed in front of her. He grabbed her arm to run with him.

They came around the house at full speed and there stood Colm.

She ran straight for him and reached out to push him back. "Bees! Come on! We have to get away!"

In her pushing, she felt him panting as though he had just exerted all his energy in doing something. In the next second, his arms tightened around her and he lifted her up and ran for the barn. She burrowed into his neck and felt the comfort he offered in this terrifying moment.

Another terrifying moment.

Gretchen lifted her head to watch the determination in his handsome face. A savior to the rescue…again.

She looked over her shoulder to the spot she'd run into his arms.

It was as though Colm knew Ethan would lead her to that exact spot and had been waiting for her.

Had they been in on this together? Did he

work in sync with his painter as he did with his cameraman?

Gretchen didn't have to look around to know the camera was rolling. But she did and sure enough, Nate approached with his camera on his shoulder.

Inside the barn Ethan reached for her and together the two men brought her to the ground. "Gretchen, your breathing sounds labored. Are you allergic to bees?"

Labored? That was when she heard the wheezing louder with every breath. The asthma attack threatening all day was in full swing.

"That's it. I'm calling 911," Colm announced and walked to Nate who handed him a phone.

"I'm…not…aller…gic," Gretchen huffed between short breaths. She needed her backup. Her last puff in the canister. Gretchen retrieved the inhaler and filled her lungs with medicine. "Asthma."

"They're on their way," Colm said with the phone to his ear, his hand rubbing the back of his head. "Hang tight, Goldie. I'm going to get to the bottom of this, today."

She didn't care if the camera was on them or not. She opened her mouth, and with a loud voice she said, "The only place you're going… is back to…jail."

* * *

Colm stood off to Ethan's side while the painter rubbed Gretchen's back. Every swirl of his hand brought on a wave of unwanted jealousy that at one point in Colm's life wouldn't have ended well for Ethan. Now, he knew enough that the feeling stirring in him didn't mean he should go a row with the guy. It only meant he wanted to be the one comforting Gretchen.

But she didn't want him anywhere near her.

"Gretchen, I had nothing to do with this," Colm said to all four pairs of ears. It was no use explaining his plight. The pain in his head made it nearly impossible anyway. He dared not mention the attack on him yet. Not without a clue as to who had knocked him out. Colm would bide his time until he had the sheriff's ear to fill. He meant it when he said he would get to the bottom of this today. But he would do it legit.

Sirens blared through the trees off in the distance, but Colm's eyes stayed focused on Gretchen. Her breathing had evened out since she'd taken the puff from her inhaler, but with her face turned away from him he couldn't be sure she was out of the woods. Regardless of her lack of trust, Colm thanked God for protecting her. *Please, Lord, continue to protect her from whatever game someone is playing here. Someone who might be standing with us right now.*

The crowd grew; more of the crew came to see what was happening. Two sheriff's department vehicles screamed into the driveway, along with an old medical service station wagon. The sheriff was taking this call seriously, and Colm liked him already for it. He stepped up to meet the clean-cut military-looking man getting out of his vehicle.

"That's the man I told you about, Sheriff," the blond-headed officer getting out of the other cruiser said. "The one who held me down."

A quick glance told him it was the deputy who'd punched him, but Colm was sure the man had left that part out. "We can talk about that later. It's Gretchen who needs help."

"I'm fine. It was just my asthma, Owen." Colm turned to find her on her feet, addressing the sheriff. Colm gave her a small smile, but she didn't return it. "I just need another inhaler. I'm all out."

"Gretchen," the sheriff said, "why don't you let Dr. Schaffer take you to the clinic to examine you?"

"No, I told you it was only my asthma. I got a few bee stings, but I'm fine. Ethan was stung, too. Maybe he needs Doc's help."

"I'm all right," Ethan said. "We got away in time."

The sheriff's passenger-side car door opened

and out stepped an older woman with a bleached-blond bouffant. She wore some type of blue authentic German dress with a white ruffled blouse. She looked like a cute older lady, except for the pure disdain she leveled at Colm. He had no idea who she was, but he knew already she didn't like him.

"Mom, what are you doing here?" Gretchen stepped up beside him, her arm brushed his, and Colm thought she might grab on. Whether she did or not, Colm would stand by in case she needed him.

"I came to ask you one more time to stop all these pipe dreams and come home." The woman's voice was gruff, and she looked used to giving orders *and* getting her way. Until now. No wonder Gretchen felt she had something to prove to her mother. She'd probably spent her whole life following orders, first from her mom, then from her boyfriend.

"With all due respect, ma'am, Gretchen will make a smart business owner. She has quite the head on her shoulders and will have a fine home right here. She's quite handy."

"Then why does she need you?"

"I don't," Gretchen said and stood away from him. It hit him straight to the heart.

"Len told me about the hole in the floor and how someone cut it," her mother went on.

"You've brought danger to this island by inviting these strangers. And now Len's painting is gone."

Gretchen lifted her head. "Gone? As in someone took it? He told me he was leaving it to me. Maybe one of the islanders grabbed it before—"

"How dare you accuse us! It disappeared right after this crew arrived. If you came to town, you would know."

"I didn't mean to sound accusing, but I also don't see how the crew would even know about it. Or want it. It only means something to Len. This has to be killing him."

"He is quite…distraught." Her mother dropped her gaze.

"How's his mind?"

Her mom shrugged. "I don't know. He doesn't seem right."

"I noticed that, too, when he came to visit me. It concerned me."

"If you cared about Len, you'd send this crew away and come home."

"Coming home is not going to change anything. Besides, this is my home now. Len accepts this—why can't you?"

"I do not have to accept anything. Other than leaving Billy, inviting this TV show here is the worst decision you have ever made. It's put everyone at risk."

Gretchen ignored her mother's jab about the breakup and said, "Nobody's been hurt."

Colm brushed her ear. "Nobody but you," he whispered. And him, but that he was keeping in his pocket for now.

Gretchen angled a quick, harsh look at him. He understood her warning to keep it all quiet.

"Does this jigsaw belong to someone in particular?" Deputy Baker approached the group holding out a familiar-looking tool.

"Where did you get that?" Colm stepped forward. "Did you go through my things without a warrant?"

"No need of a warrant. Found it lying in the grass by the ladder, right out in the open. But it's interesting how well you know the law. Learn the rules so you can get around them?"

"My jigsaw is in my bucket. That can't be mine."

"It is your jigsaw," Gretchen said, her voice heavy with contempt. "I brought it out to show you the proof."

"Proof of what?"

"Do you always treat your equipment with such carelessness? Or did you not realize you bent the blade when you cut my floor?"

Colm jerked at her accusation. He studied her face for any sign of disbelief in what she was saying. Nothing. "Let me see the jigsaw," he said to Deputy Baker.

"No can do." Sheriff Matthews spoke up. "The tool could be evidence. We'll have to match the blade cuts in the floor to find out. Run some tests on wood particles, as well. Mr. McCrae, would you mind coming to the station to answer some questions? Away from so many eyes?"

"Wait, you're arresting him?" Gretchen's eyes showed remorse.

Colm breathed a sigh of relief. She hadn't lost all hope in him yet.

"No, Gretchen, he can't arrest me. He doesn't have any evidence that shows a crime has occurred. And even if he does, he's not going to find anything that points to me. Even if that blade turns out to be the one used to cut your floorboards, that doesn't mean I did it." Colm looked straight at the sheriff. "And he knows it. He just wants to talk. And that's okay because I have a few things I want to share with him, too."

Colm reached for Gretchen's arm as he had wanted to when she stepped up beside him. Her hand came over his but thankfully, she didn't push him away. Instead he felt her grasp tighten, and he felt her fear.

"I'll be back in a few hours. Ethan!" Colm called without taking his eyes off her.

"I got it covered," Ethan announced from the crowd of onlookers, exactly what Colm wanted to hear. No other directions needed. His painter would watch over her.

Colm released Gretchen. He leaned in and brushed his cheek against hers, his lips close to her ear. "Keep your eyes and ears open, Goldie. And call the sheriff for any reason. I mean it. No more bravado."

At her single nod, he knew she finally understood the risks, and this wasn't a time to prove her independence.

"And let the EMT look you over. It doesn't make you weak."

He stepped away and entered the backseat of the cruiser. Sheriff Matthews climbed in and put the car into Reverse. As the car backed out of the driveway, Colm watched Gretchen get smaller through the windshield. Before they met the road, Billy Baker stepped up beside her. She cringed and shrugged away, right into Troy. She shrank back as though she feared that man more than Billy.

Colm wondered if he'd missed something between the two of them. He straightened up in the seat, ready to tell Sheriff Matthews to stop the car. But Ethan appeared right behind Gretchen and Colm relaxed a bit. The painter would do as he said and watch out for her.

A twinge of jealousy swirled in Colm's gut at his once again not being the one by her side. But even if he hadn't been in the cruiser on his way to an interrogation, Gretchen didn't trust him any more than she trusted anyone else. Colm vowed to change that as soon as possible. For now she would be safe with Ethan.

Plus, he had an attack of his own to report to the sheriff. Not that he'd seen the face of his assailant, but he did see the color green.

Green…

Colm whipped his head to his right as Sheriff Matthews pulled the car down the street. He craned to see the men beside Gretchen.

Deputy Billy Baker wore a green deputy's uniform. Colm passed over Ethan's paint-splattered jersey and noticed Troy wore a dark green suit.

Colm looked at Ethan and willed him to protect her today, but on a closer look at the painter, Colm could make out the shirt color under the splatter of other paint colors.

Green.

SEVEN

"Show's closed," Deputy Billy Baker announced as though he had all the authority in the world. "The renovation is over. You're all going back to where you came from. Today."

Gretchen watched in disbelief, but also in the same quiet position she always assumed when her ex took control. The same silent acceptance as when he'd said she *should* stay home and not go to college…as when he told her who her friends should be, even if that meant turning her back on her lifelong best friend when she needed Gretchen most. So much silence for so long. Even after she finally broke it off and endured his angry retaliation, she'd kept her mouth shut.

"No more." The words spilled from her lips at first in a whisper, then louder. "No more. Do you hear me, Billy Baker?" Gretchen stepped forward to go after him as he turned the corner of the house and left the eyes of the crowd. "Everyone, do not pack up. We continue this renovation as scheduled. He can't stop us." Gretchen sped past them. She caught up with Billy at his car and reached out to grab his arm. "I will not let you dictate how I live my life anymore. We are over, and I will not keep silent about who you really are anymore."

Billy yanked his arm away, nearly sending her flying around him. He faced her head-on, leaning in with more menace than she had ever seen. "You will do what I say, or you will regret it." He lifted the backside of his hand to her cheek. "Do I need to remind you how you made me lose my cool the last time?"

"Threaten me all you want. It's not going to stop me from telling everyone how you hurt me."

Quick as lightning, Billy retracted his hand only to let it fly back into her face with a force that lifted her off the ground and sent her sailing.

Stunned as she lay in the gravel of her driveway, Gretchen held her stinging face. Half her brain said, *Get back up.* The other half said, *Don't move.*

She couldn't voice the words as she had said out back, but she still could hear them in her mind.

No more.

Gretchen got to her knees. She put her weight

on one foot, then the other. Slowly, she pushed herself up as straight as she could. It wasn't perfect, but it felt so good. The last time, she had remained on the floor and shook with stunned fear. She wouldn't be lying down anymore.

"Coming back for more?" Billy lifted a curled fist, his college ring shiny and huge on his finger. She stared at it, knowing he would most likely plow it in her face next. Would she even be able to get back up again?

She had to. No matter what.

"Help me!" Gretchen tried to scream, but by Billy's laugh, she was pretty sure she only squeaked.

Billy reached for her with both hands.

"Cut," a voice came from the side of the house loud and clear. Both of them twisted to see the huge camera being carried closer.

Nate had captured the whole scene on film?

Relief swept over Gretchen. "Oh, thank God," she cried. "And thank you, Nate. Now everyone will know the truth. Now they'll believe me."

Billy raced for Nate. "Give me that film," he demanded.

"No can do. All footage belongs to the boss. And I'm sure the sheriff would like a look. Are you all right, Gretchen?" Nate asked with Billy blocking his view to her.

"Yes. Everything's going to be all right now. Thank you."

"That's what you think." Billy shot a lethal look her way. He turned back to Nate. "Hand over the film, or I will see to it that you are arrested."

"For what? I haven't done anything."

"For whatever I plant on you. You don't know who you're messing with."

"You just said that in front of a witness. I'm really not afraid."

"Dead witnesses don't talk."

Gretchen's legs stiffened at Billy's implied words. Any doubts she had about his innocence in the accidents were erased. He meant for her to die?

She had to move. She had to get away from this madman. Gretchen ran to her front-porch steps and took them at high speed. She flung her front door wide and pushed through blindly, slamming into a man's chest.

"There you are. You disappeared on me. I came in to look for you. Where've you been?"

Gretchen backed away and saw Ethan with so much concern flooding his eyes she nearly wept.

"Colm asked me to watch out for you. Don't take off like that again. I really don't want to get on his bad side. He seems like the type to spike a bad temper if provoked." Ethan smiled down at her. "Promise?"

Gretchen couldn't speak yet, but she could nod.

"Good. You really scared me with that asthma attack. You feel all right now?"

She touched her cheek and winced, her asthma the least of her concerns. "Been better," she whispered. How was one supposed to feel when they just learned their ex wanted them dead?

"I'm sure, but not to worry." Ethan took her hand and gave it a squeeze. "You're safe with me. And I'm not going anywhere."

"You have nothing to hold me here overnight with!" Colm yelled at the mirror on the wall of the sheriff's interrogation room. "And leaving me in here alone for hours isn't helping Gretchen."

His hands tapped restlessly on the metal desk he sat at. It had been cold to the touch when he first arrived, but after the sun went down and his body temp escalated from frustration, the whole room heated up. Nothing Colm said to Sheriff Matthews seemed to make a difference. The man didn't believe him that his deputy was the danger around here. "Can you at least tell me where Deputy Baker is? Was he the one who struck me over the head in the basement? Have you asked him where he was at the time?"

No answer.

The tactic of isolation didn't seem like the sheriff's MO, so something else had to be keeping the lawman. Visions of Gretchen fighting for her life came to mind.

"Please, Sheriff, I need to know if she's well. That she's safe. That I didn't leave her in the care of someone who might hurt her." Colm rested his head on the table, praying that Ethan was a good guy.

The door opened and Colm shot out of his chair. It fell back onto the floor with an echoing clatter. He barely heard it as he waited for Sheriff Matthews to speak.

"Sit back down, McCrae," Sheriff Matthews instructed as he came around the other side of the table for his own chair.

"I can't. I've been sitting for hours. I've told you everything I can, and then some. You have to let me go. I've done nothing wrong."

Sheriff Matthews wasn't going to agree. Colm could see it on his face.

"If anything happens to her, I'll—"

The sheriff halted his words with a raised hand. "Don't go threatening me. I'll be able to keep you a lot longer than twenty-four hours.

We have laws here about assaulting an officer of the law."

Colm frowned. "I see my old life precedes me. The repercussions of the poor choices I once made will follow me forever, I suppose. But, Sheriff, I wasn't going to threaten you. I was going to say, if anything happens to her, I'll never forgive myself. End of story."

Sheriff Matthews cringed. "I apologize. That was judgmental of me. Sometimes the weight of my job to protect this island almost single-handedly clouds my vision. My wife will give me a talking-to, you can be sure." He walked around the table and picked up the overturned chair. "Please, sit. We need to talk."

Colm longed for the door, but any opposition would only prolong his getting back to Gretchen. "Can you just tell me if she's well? Then I'll sit."

"I just spoke to her. She's fine. Getting ready to turn out the lights." Sheriff Matthews looked at the chair with a nod of invitation.

Colm grabbed the back rung and took the seat.

"You seem to care about her." Sheriff Matthews sat and leaned in.

"I shouldn't, but I do."

"Why shouldn't you? Are you putting her in danger by caring for her?"

"She's already in danger." Colm stopped, not wanting to speak for Gretchen or spill about her abuse at the hands of the sheriff's own deputy. It was her story to tell. But he also couldn't be vague if he meant to get out of here and back to her tonight. "You need to talk to Gretchen. And you need to listen to her. Trust her when she tells you things that you may not want to hear."

"Like what?"

Colm pressed his lips tight.

"Does this have anything to do with Billy?"

Colm bit down hard on his lower lip. He thought of his mother and how she never wanted anyone to know—even though everyone did. They just pretended they didn't, because that was how she wanted it. She'd made it clear when she turned her own son away that night. There was nothing else to do but to leave and let her keep her secret.

"It's hard to watch atrocities in life when you can't do anything to stop them," Colm said. "The fact is you can't help anyone with your hands tied."

Sheriff Matthews's chest rose and fell. "You're not going to tell me, are you?"

Colm shook his head in answer. "Speak to Gretchen."

"Give me something, McCrae. I've got an island in upheaval, and with you being the new guy with a sordid past, all fingers point to you. Give me something to put the light on someone else. Otherwise you're spending the night."

Colm swallowed hard. Revealing Gretchen's secret wasn't his place. "What kind of man would I be, Sheriff, if I dishonored Gretchen's wishes and spoke for her? I'll take the night in jail if I have to."

"You're okay with that?"

"It won't be the first time I took the jail cell over spilling someone's secrets. My own mother asked me to do the same thing to protect her abusing husband. I spent my teenage years trying to wrap my head around the reasons she would protect him, but the fact is that bond is powerful…"

"Are you saying Gretchen was abused and she's still protecting this person?"

"I didn't say anything about Gretchen. I said my mother."

Sheriff Matthews nodded slowly. "I see. And your…mother, she protected someone who abused her?"

"Still is to this day."

"Why not tell the world so it will stop?"

"Because then she would have to admit to her weaknesses and her choices. After all, she's allowed the abuse to continue. It's part of the bond, the guilt put on her as though she's to blame. She feels responsible and thinks she needs to pay for her involvement."

Silence cloaked the room. Suddenly, Sheriff Matthews pushed his chair back and stood.

Colm followed his every move to the door. "Where are you off to?"

He opened the door wide. "I have a deputy to find. Sit tight until I confirm a few details."

"Sheriff," Colm said, standing, "let me return to Gretchen's side to protect her while you do."

"What if, like your mother, Gretchen doesn't want your protection? Maybe your mother saw something in you that made her think it was best for you to go away."

Colm's stomach clenched at the shot. He felt his legs give out and he sank back into the chair on a huff. "Maybe you're right." A light bulb in his mind flashed bright. "I'd become an animal, and she knew I would fight him to the death. Either of ours."

"That's why I think you should stay here." Sheriff Matthews stepped through the door and closed it softly.

Colm stared at it while his past deeds went through his head. Then he said, "But I'm different now. I'm a new creation in Christ. My old self is dead." Colm dropped his gaze to his hands, hating what he saw. They were fisted in his lap, looking ready for a fight. "My old self is dead...isn't it?"

Gretchen lay in her bed and studied the schedule in her planner. Three weeks until opening, the starred date reminded her, but all she could think about was Colm.

She shot a glance out her window to where sporadic trailer lights lit up her usually dark woods. Slowly, lights flickered off as each crew member settled in for the night—each crew member except for Colm.

Sheriff Matthews had called and said he would probably keep him for the night until Billy corroborated a few things Colm had told him.

At first words of injustice sprang to her lips, then panic choked them out and all she could ask was what kinds of things had Colm mentioned.

Owen wanted to know if Billy had struck Colm in self-defense out at the rock or if the deputy had used unwarranted force. The sheriff referred to Colm, but he also asked if Billy had used force on anyone else, as well.

The question lingered over the line before she answered.

Gretchen told him the truth...about Colm. She wanted to say more about Billy's "unwarranted force" against her, but the words wouldn't come. Not over the phone, she'd told herself; she settled for making sure Colm's character was protected this night instead.

She had to wonder if anyone ever considered that Colm had a character to protect. He'd told her he had changed, but people had a way of reminding you of your old character...or expecting you to be that same person when you never wanted to be again.

She understood this firsthand.

Gretchen placed her planner on the nightstand and faced the vast sky of stars through the window. "Lord, I think I know what Colm feels like. He wants to change, but people will always point out his past. I wanted the same thing, but the people in my life were also stuck in the past. It hurt me, but today I was no better. I accused Colm of cutting the floor. I jumped right at him without even asking him. Forgive me and help me to see the real Colm. The man he is today. The real man he wants to be."

Gretchen watched the last trailer light flicker out. As she reached for the switch on her lamp, it powered out on its own, leaving her in complete darkness. She turned the switch anyway, but nothing happened. The lack of red numbers on her alarm clock told her the power was out.

"You've got to be kidding me." She sighed in frustration. The house may have an updated electrical box, but the wiring running through the walls was still ancient. Who knew when she'd be able to get the power up and running? She'd have to switch over to the generator for now.

She climbed out of bed and put her feet into her slippers. She really did not want to go down into the dark basement. Could it wait until morning? she wondered. Probably, but what kind of home owner would that make her?

She reached the stairs just as a sound from above caught her attention.

Her ear caught another sound. Some sort of creak, but it could very well be an old-house sound.

Or it could be Ethan. He'd said he would keep an eye on the place during the night. He was taking his promise to Colm to watch over her seriously.

"Ethan," she called out, "are you still here?"

No answer.

She walked toward the end of the hall to the room with the walkup attic entrance. "Are you upstairs?"

The attic door stood open. Approaching it, she peered up into darkness. "Hello?"

A strange smell wafted down to her, causing her to scrunch her nose. Moonlight streamed through the windows, casting shadows on the wooden floors, but upstairs the small gable windows wouldn't shed much light. Should she check things out in the darkness?

Once again she asked, what kind of home owner was she? She had made the choice to take on this huge house all by herself. Calling someone to check on every squeak and creak she heard in the night wasn't an option.

With her mind made up, she took the stairs.

Gretchen reached the top landing and found the sweet odor even more pronounced. Pine trees and licorice. It reminded her of the stuff she used to clean paintbrushes.

She sniffed.

Turpentine. Had Ethan been up here painting tonight? "Ethan," she called again. "Are you up here?"

With no answer and only the stars as light to search through the rooms, Gretchen went back to the stairs.

Only the door below was now closed.

Gretchen's heart skipped a beat. "Hey!" She felt her way down the steps in the pitch-dark. Her foot slipped down two treads before she caught the railing. She reached out blindly until she collided with the door, feeling for the door-knob.

Locked.

"Ethan! Are you out there?" she shouted.

"Anybody?" Her voice hitched. Her breathing picked up. It took her a moment before she realized she wasn't getting full breaths.

"No, no, no, no," she said in a panic. She couldn't be having another asthmatic episode so quickly.

The wheezing said otherwise.

This was a full-blown attack. Two in one day after months of having none. Why? Not important. Getting it under control was all that mattered. But how could she do this without an inhaler? Even if she wasn't locked in the attic, she'd used her last puff this afternoon.

Gretchen tried to steady her breaths. She forced her mind to focus on breathing in through her nose, but the strong piney smell assaulted her senses so that her wheezing deepened.

She realized that the odor was bringing on the attack. It was the toxicity of the turpentine! If she didn't escape quickly, it would only get worse until…

Gretchen banged repeatedly on the door. There was no way any of the crew would hear her in their trailers, but was Ethan still around?

Gretchen turned and raced up the stairs, first on her hands and knees to feel her way, but the smell was so strong closer to the floor that she stood to get away from it.

Someone had poured the solvent all the way

up the stairs. After all that had happened to her, she knew she shouldn't be surprised, but in her piercing pain and the horrendous sounds coming from her throat she had to admit someone wanted her to suffer. *Cruel* didn't describe this attack. *Sinister* came closer.

Dirty was even better.

But Colm did not do this. He was at the sheriff's department for the night. And he wasn't even here to play the chivalrous knight come to her rescue.

Right about now she would have taken that, camera and all.

Her breaths shortened to squeaking fragments. The only word to describe this awful act would be *murder.*

She was going to die.

Gretchen reached the top step. She fell to her hands and knees and looked up to the two windows high up in the gables. Too high to reach. But maybe she could climb up onto something. Something big enough, but not too heavy to move beneath one of the windows.

Gretchen crawled around, her heart plummeting as she felt nothing but open space. Not even small objects to throw at the windows to break them.

Oh, how she wished she could break just one window to ventilate the room. The starry sky above taunted her with the cool evening air on the other side of the glass. Tears sprang from her eyes in frustration and fear. She'd been successfully taken to her knees, right where someone wanted her. But *who*?

Billy had threatened her earlier, but when would he have come up here to douse the place? She'd been alone upstairs all night, and Ethan would have seen someone come through the doors downstairs.

Gretchen couldn't give up. She had to keep looking as long as she had one breath left. She crawled back around, using the moonlight shadows as a guide, then saw an area where no light shone. Thinking perhaps she'd find something to throw, she dragged her slowing body into the darkness.

A few crawls in, her body dropped as her chest convulsed in sharp pains. She couldn't go any farther. She swept her hand out in one direction to feel around her. Nothing. She pulled her body a little more and swept her arm again. The tips of her fingers brushed against something hard. Hope flourished, but she'd have to move her body even more to feel what it was and try to lift it to throw.

I can do this. I won't let whoever's trying to hurt me keep me down. I can do this!

Gretchen repeated her silent words as she

reached again and touched the object with more than her fingertips. First her knuckles then the palm of her hand found the object.

It was too large to throw. Before she let her hope deflate with her lungs, she thought maybe it would be tall enough to climb up onto *if* she could move it toward the window. She had to try.

Agony ripped through her chest as she got to her knees and leaned against a wooden chest. She pushed uselessly with her weakened arms, then turned her shoulder into it to use the weight of her body. A few heaves and flashes of light blinked in her eyes. She pushed again and her body fell forward, slumped against the box.

Gretchen used her elbows to get back up and pushed with all her might. Wood scraped and she fell again, but this time it was because she'd moved the chest forward.

Hope blossomed again even as the last air in her lungs dispersed. She gave another shove. The chest shifted and for a split second more hope gave her a boost of energy.

Then the chest came to a stop. In the dark she couldn't tell what halted it. Possibly a raised floorboard. Whatever it was, this was the end of the line.

And the end of her.

In frustration she cried out a distorted, raspy sound she'd never made before. A sound that would mark the end of her life, and she would never know who did this to her.

Billy? Troy? Colm?

Or maybe it was Len!

If she could, she would have laughed at that thought. It must have been the lack of oxygen to her brain. Len would never hurt her.

But he had been up in the attic the day the crew arrived. Had the town's patriarch turned on her, too? Had he lied to her when he said he was on her side? He could have poured the turpentine when he was here. Maybe he was more upset about her turning Stepping Stones into a tourist location than he let on. Maybe he believed she was ruining his precious island and had to stop her. He may not have the physical strength to stop her, but it didn't take much muscle to pour turpentine in a closed space and attack her at her weakest point.

Gretchen didn't know what hurt her heart more, the asthma attack or the idea she was being killed by the man who was the only grandfather she'd ever known. She grabbed the top of the chest to try and pull herself up onto it, but her movement caused the chest to fall toward her with a thump. The hinged lid swung wide. Hard, heavy articles fell out on her.

Books. Her hands confirmed the hardback volumes. At first she thought them useless. Then she saw the stars through the glass. The fresh air on the other side awaited her if she could break through.

Gretchen lifted the heavy book and hurled it up, shattering the glass into tinkling pieces.

Now what?

It wasn't as if she had any way to reach the fresh air beyond it. All Gretchen could do was lie on the floor, her head back, watching the expanse of sky. The last sky she would ever see.

Her breaths were shallow and useless now. The agonizing wheezes sounded more like the squeaks of a small mouse. Her body still worked to keep her alive, but it wouldn't be long before it gave up.

Gretchen closed her eyes. It took effort she didn't have to keep them open. Darkness prevailed and some part of her brain said it was over.

She felt a light touch on her shoulder. Her body flinched but couldn't react in any other way. Not even when she felt her body being scooped up into strong, male arms.

The first name that came to her was Colm, but that didn't make sense. Colm wasn't here. But then who was it? Did Ethan come back to help her as he'd promised? Or was it…Billy?

Panic raced through her befuddled mind and she tried to push away from the man's hold. Her eyes fluttered open but not enough to get a clear image. Whoever carried her may be taking her out to the fresh air to save her, or taking her out to the ocean to dump her.

EIGHT

Colm leaned back against the mirrored wall, rolling his head side to side in a movement as useless as he felt. He'd tried sitting but that lasted all of thirty seconds. How could he sit knowing Gretchen needed defending?

What?

When had his desire changed from protecting her to defending her? She would be the first to shut him down, saying she would take care of herself. Her independence was crucial to her identity. She wanted nothing from anybody, including him. At least he didn't have to worry about her going back to her abuser as he had with his mother. But that didn't mean Gretchen's abuser wouldn't come looking for her.

The door burst wide with Sheriff Matthews behind it. "Let's go."

Colm raced to the door. He didn't have to ask if it was bad. Sheriff Matthews's tight, stricken face expressed it all. "Where is she?" Colm asked.

"At the clinic. Someone left her out front. She's unconscious. Bad asthma attack."

"Or made to look like it, you mean." Colm picked up his steps. He followed the sheriff through the hall and into the main lobby of the department. But out the front door, his feet halted on the crushed-seashell walkway.

"To the right," Sheriff Matthews instructed as the two started running together. "Two doors down."

Two doors, but at least a thousand yards. The buildings held plenty of space between them. Ordinarily that would be a nice feature of the island, but not at the moment. He wanted to be in that clinic and beside Gretchen this instant.

"Who found her?" Colm asked.

"Doctor Schaffer. He found her lying against the glass doors and took her right in."

"I doubt she walked herself there."

"Maybe whoever dropped her off didn't want the fame for saving her."

"Yeah, right. More like they didn't want to be fingered as a suspect."

"As far as we know it was an asthma attack. Nothing more." Sheriff Matthews ran under the streetlight and Colm caught the look of doubt on his face.

The lantern light in front of the clinic beamed like a beacon leading their way up to the front glass doors. Sheriff Matthews entered first and held up a hand to stop Colm.

"Tildy's already here and may not think too kindly of you coming in. Be prepared for her to throw you out. You're not family."

Colm didn't like it one bit, but the sheriff was correct. What was he to Gretchen other than the TV show host for her renovation? And yet, he couldn't be anywhere else but by her side.

Tildy stepped out of a room off the lobby. She started. "Why is he here? Haven't he and his crew done enough damage? How do we know he didn't cause this?"

The sheriff said, "Colm's been in custody all day and night." He cast a quick glance Colm's way. "Besides, I have reason to believe Gretchen is in danger from someone who lives on the island."

"Don't be ridiculous. Is that what he told you? I'm surprised at you, Sheriff. You should know when someone is pulling the wool over your eyes to cover his own crimes." Tildy turned to Colm. "You might as well leave. There's not a chance I'm going to let you see her."

"I respect your decision, Mum, but I'm not leaving." Colm walked to a chair in the waiting room and sat down. "If this is as close as I can be to her, then this is where I will stay."

Tildy and Sheriff Matthews exchanged looks

of heated silence before he asked, "How is she? Has she woken up?"

Tildy hesitated, then nodded. "Briefly. Doctor Schaffer gave her oxygen to clear her airways, but my baby girl was so wiped out physically, she fell asleep right away."

"Did she say anything when she came to? About what happened?"

Tildy shook her head and stared at the plant in the corner of the waiting room.

"Did she name any names?"

Tildy jutted her head at Colm. "His."

"Mine?" Colm's heart lurched in his chest. He swallowed the pain of Gretchen's believing even for a second he'd harmed her. "She thought I did this to her?"

Tildy pursed her lips and crossed her arms at her chest. "She thought you rescued her."

"Did she say anything else? Mention anyone else?" Sheriff Matthews asked.

A hanging thread on her pink robe became the woman's focus.

"Tildy, who else did she mention?"

"Billy," she whispered.

"What about Billy?"

"Sheriff." Her whisper became desperate. "I think… I don't want it to be true, but she seemed afraid of him." Tildy sniffed and swallowed. "Have we been wrong about him?"

Sheriff Matthews looked at Colm, but Colm was doing all he could not to react. *Help me, Lord, to stay calm. I will be no help to Gretchen if I revert to my old ways.*

"Mom?" a fragile voice said from the other room. "Mom, are you still here?"

Colm jumped from his seat but at Tildy's glare, he stopped. He'd have to deal with the torture of watching Tildy and Sheriff Matthews enter the room, when all he wanted to do was bowl them over and rush to Gretchen's side.

Returning to his seat wasn't an option, either. Colm stood outside the door to listen to her voice. She'd sounded as weak as a kitten. So not like her.

Come on, Goldie, where's your neart istigh? Colm rested his forehead on the wall by her door, willing Gretchen's inner strength to return. He needed to know she hadn't been broken down completely. He needed to hear it to keep him from hunting down Billy Baker tonight.

Clean oxygen flowed freely into Gretchen's lungs, each breath a gift she'd never take for granted again. She opened her eyes to find her mom at her bedside. The worry etched on her face took Gretchen back years to when her father died. The message her mom sent was clear that day: *We won't survive without him.* For a long time Gretchen had tried to prove her mother wrong, but it caused strife between them. Strife that only ended when she went on her first date with Billy.

"Who did this to you?" her mom asked as she brushed her hand across Gretchen's cheek. Her touch stung and Gretchen flinched.

Then she remembered why it hurt. Billy had hit her. *By now there must be a bruise.*

There was no hiding anything now.

Gretchen opened her mouth to tell all, but her throat closed right up. Why was admitting this weakness so hard to do?

"You need to tell us what happened."

"Us?" Gretchen lifted her head to scan the room. Was Colm sitting beside her?

"The sheriff and me, of course. Who did you think I meant? Billy?"

Gretchen inhaled sharply, unable to stop the response even with the pain it caused in her chest. "Is he here?" She tried to push up, but her mom settled a hand on her shoulder.

"Would you want him to be?"

Gretchen looked at Sheriff Matthews in the doorway, then back at her mom. Why did she get the feeling they already knew who put the bruise on her face? Slowly, Gretchen shook her head. Tears pooled in her eyes. "He hurt me,

Mom." She looked down, away from the disappointment on her mother's face.

Her mother's hand touched her beneath her chin and lifted it back up. "You have nothing to be ashamed of. I've been a fool. I pushed too hard. I wanted him so badly for you. I wanted you to have what I had with your father. I wanted to believe Billy would take care of you as your dad did me. With this independence tirade you've always been on, I was so afraid you would end up alone. When you broke it off with Billy, I thought you were back on your soapbox again. Never did I think he…"

"So, Billy did assault you?" Sheriff Matthews asked as he approached the foot of the bed. "He gave you that bruise on your face?"

A deep, ugly growl came from outside the doorway.

Gretchen tried to look behind Sheriff Matthews. "Who's out there? Is that Billy? Are you ganging up on me again?"

Her mother patted her shoulder, but Gretchen shrugged it off. "Sweetheart, it's not Billy."

"Then who is it?"

Sheriff Matthews faced her mother. "Tildy, I'm calling this shot." At Tildy's reluctant nod, he continued, "Colm, you're welcome to join—" Colm rushed in and right past the sheriff "—us now."

"Colm," Gretchen said as she reached for the hand he placed on her good cheek. His eyes had yet to meet hers. Instead, they searched her face, always returning to the injured side. "I'm okay." She tried to grab his attention with her eyes. "Just grand." She said it just as he would say it, accent and all.

The only thing he noticed was her face. "What happened?"

"It was an asthma attack."

"Asthma attacks don't leave bruises. Was it Billy or Ethan who put that there?"

"Ethan? No, Billy h-hit—" She choked and wondered if the confession would ever come easy. "Why would Ethan hurt me?"

"I hadn't thought he would when I asked him to watch over you, but I was knocked over the head in the basement and all I saw was the color green. Billy's deputy uniform is green, but under all Ethan's paint splatters, he was also wearing a green shirt. Troy's suit had green in it, too, for that matter, so I'm not thinking I'll be able to identify my attacker anytime soon. But—"

"Wait. Stop. You were hit?" Gretchen used her elbows to hoist herself up against the pillow. "Are you okay?"

"No need to worry, love. I have a hard head."

"How can I not? You were obviously hurt because of me. I won't allow this to happen. You're a guest on this island and here to help me."

"You've allowed yourself to be hurt, but can't allow it for me? I don't understand your logic. Explain it to me, Gretchen."

Gretchen threw a glance at her mom. "I can't explain it. Part of me didn't believe I deserved to be under Billy's control, but I still stayed in the relationship."

Tildy sniffed. "Because of me."

"No, Mom. It was my choice to stay." Gretchen looked back at Colm. "But I told, Colm. There's no more secrets to hold me down anymore." Her lips trembled. "It's over now. It's really over. I'm so sorry you had to get hurt before I told. If only—"

"Nay. No more blame. Now it's time to stand strong again. I know you have it in you, Gretchen. I've seen it. But I am glad to hear my painter had nothing to do with putting you in this bed."

"Ethan didn't hurt me. In fact, he was there for me after Billy did. He did exactly what you wanted him to do. He offered me comfort when I felt very alone and scared."

Colm frowned. "That's not exactly what I asked him to do… Never mind. I was worried. I imagined every scenario out there happening to you, but seeing you in this clinic because of Billy's fists…"

"No. It wasn't fists that put me here." Gretchen set the record straight. "Someone poured turpentine in the attic."

"Turpentine?" said all three people surrounding her.

"That's what caused my asthma attack. I got locked in the attic, and the fumes were too much with no ventilation."

"You got locked in, or someone locked you in?" Colm asked.

"I don't know, but…"

"But what?"

"I thought I heard a noise. It's an old house, though. I could be wrong. I'm second-guessing everything right now—even my plans to move forward with owning a home. But that's exactly what Billy wants. I feel like I'm falling right into his trap. Maybe Billy did put me in this bed. He did insinuate that he was going to kill me after he struck me, Sheriff. Can you arrest him on that?"

"I'll bring him in for assaulting you, of course. According to you and Colm, I've hired an abuser as a deputy, which means his profession is on the line in addition to his freedom. But there'll need to be an investigation on the turpentine. I particularly would like to know who delivered you to the clinic and will ask around to see if anyone saw anything."

Gretchen nodded absently. Something about Sheriff Matthews's words rubbed her wrong. "Nate filmed Billy hitting me. Thank God he was there, and for once the camera came in handy. Although now Billy might go after *him*."

Sheriff Matthews's expression darkened. "That could be dangerous for Nate. I'll make it a point to see him first. I've called Detective Wesley Grant and his forensic scientist wife, Lydia, to come over from the mainland for assistance, but they won't be here until the morning. Daybreak can't get here fast enough. Without Billy, I'm now a one-man show."

Gretchen still thought on Sheriff Matthews's previous words. "I'm sorry, Sheriff. Did you say Colm told you about Billy being an abuser?" She turned to the man still holding her hand. She felt her own begin to sweat beneath his grasp. "You told the sheriff about Billy? How he treated me? How could you?"

Colm's face blanched.

Gretchen pushed his hand away. "You spilled my secrets to save yourself?"

"He didn't tell me, Gretchen," Sheriff Matthews inserted. "It wasn't like that. In fact he was willing to stay the night in jail to keep your secret safe. I already had my suspicions."

She shook her head. "*You've* had suspicions? Since the day the crew arrived, I've been living and breathing suspicions. I can't trust anyone."

"You can trust me," Colm confirmed loud and clear.

She shook her head. "I'm not so sure. Everything about you is staged."

Colm's mouth fell open for a split second. He snapped it shut with narrowing eyes. "Goldie, I've done my best to protect you. I'm sorry if I messed up—"

"*Protect me?* Since the day I met you, I've been falling on my face, and what have you been doing? Getting it all on film. I wouldn't be surprised if there was a camera rolling in the attic last night as I grasped for my pitiful last breaths. Tell me, Colm, will I see footage of my blue lips on primetime television? It's interesting how every time you swoop in to save the day, the camera's rolling. Everyone's favorite Irish hero saving the dumb home owner."

Colm's complexion washed white as a June moon. He swallowed hard. His blue eyes glistened. "Pitiful...blue... Oh, Gretchen, I am so sorry, love," he whispered rapidly. "I'm sorry you had to endure that agony. I should have been there."

"Why, so you could save me on film again?"

"No, of course not. I never wanted the camera filming any of your attacks. And if there was a camera in the attic last night, someone is going to pay."

"Send the camera away for the rest of the rehab, and *maybe* I'll believe you."

"I would if I could, but—"

"But you're not in charge. I get it. You may be the host, but you answer to your puppet master just as I had to answer to mine. It's tough, I know. But you can fight back, Colm."

"Fight? You want me to fight back? I promised God never to fight again."

"There are other ways to fight than with your fists. You want to help me? Don't worry about protecting me. Finish my house. Because that's the only way I'm going to win my fight."

A smile slowly appeared on his lips. Then he grabbed Gretchen's hand and brought it to his lips for a quick kiss. "You got it, Goldie. And while I'm at it, I'm going to prove that you can trust me, too." Colm nodded to Sheriff Matthews and to her mother.

"Mum, I'm going to tell you something for nothing. Your daughter is one amazing woman. She's going to prove this whole town wrong with that beautiful brain of hers." He started for the door but called at the doorway, "And, Gretchen, going forward, I better never hear you call yourself dumb again."

The front-entrance bell chimed and Gretchen rested her head back on her pillow with a sigh. "Well, that does it. If that man turns out to be a fraud, my heart won't be able to take it."

NINE

"Let me get this straight. You're willing to pay me to stop the show?" Disbelief laced Troy's voice. At Colm's nod, he let out a hoot of laughter that reached the rafters of the barn. They'd met here because the house was off-limits after Gretchen's attack last night. The sheriff had declared the place a crime scene, and they'd all woken to yellow police tape crisscrossing all the doors. No one was to enter until the house had been processed this morning by the detective and his wife from the mainland.

Troy's chuckle died down. "McCrae, a certain golden-haired beauty is about to send me down one of your rainbows right into my biggest payday ever. You don't have enough to make me walk."

"Which you would know since you drew up my crooked contract."

"That you signed willingly. Shall we reminisce about the day I offered you the 'chance of a lifetime'? Your words, not mine."

"A hungry belly tends to make a guy blind, but it also makes one frugal. I've been saving my money since day one. Nearly every penny." A wave of regret doused him, but deep down Colm knew it wouldn't matter how much he saved. Money wasn't the key to unlocking his mother's chains. "In fact, with investments, I've made your pittance grow tenfold. So just name your figure."

Troy stilled in the barn's early-morning light. He pushed his hands into his suit pants pockets. "Well, now, isn't this impressive. I'll admit I'm tempted to play your game just to see how heavy your wallet is."

"What's stopping you? Later this morning the sheriff will determine a crime has occurred here. He could shut down the renovation for the time being, and you won't receive any compensation. I suggest you take my offer and walk away with something."

Troy eyed him. He pulled his hand out of his pocket to rub his chin. "What is it about her that has you offering to break your piggy bank?"

"Easy. I put the money aside to set someone free. It might as well be Gretchen."

Troy dropped his hand and brought his arms to cross at his chest. "I don't like what you're implying."

"You're the one who draws up the contracts. Your words, not mine."

"And I hold everyone to every word in them. My answer's no to your offer. You see, Colm, we both have our investments, and I'm not going anywhere until I claim mine right here on this island." Troy's smile sickened Colm's stomach. What was the man saying? What investment?

He looked at his egotistical boss who got whatever he wanted...or else.

Was Colm staring at the man responsible for Gretchen's attacks? "Something tells me you're not talking about the show. Just how far would you go to protect your investments, Troy?" Colm stepped up to his boss.

A woman's shout drifted to the barn.

"Oh, look who's arrived home." Troy still wore his sick smile. "Shall we go say top o' the morning to her?"

Colm wanted nothing more than to wipe Troy's smug look off his face, but another, more shrieking shout came their way that hit Colm in the heart.

Colm burst out the doors. He knew Troy was

behind him, but not in any rush. The crew members came out of their trailers at the same time.

Gretchen ran straight for Colm from the porch. "I'm ruined!" she shouted. "My house! It's destroyed!"

Tears flowed down her face in rivers. She couldn't seem to focus even a second to look at him. Her hands in her hair, she paced, her footing as unsure as the rest of her. "It's ruined!" she wailed. "*I'm* ruined."

"Take it slow," Colm coaxed her. "Speak to me, Gretchen."

"There's no way… no way I'll ever open now. It's over. Forever."

Colm wasn't going to get a clear answer out of her. Whatever occurred in her home had sent her over the edge. He headed for her porch steps. The sheriff and two other people, probably the reinforcements he'd called in last night, tried to hold him back. But Gretchen had left the door wide open, and one glance through the yellow tape knocked the air right from his lungs.

Walls gouged down to their studs gaped with plaster dust coating every square foot. Colm didn't have to go any farther to know the whole house resembled the foyer, especially with the message the vandal left behind. Painted in bloodred on the floor right past the threshold: *Hand over the painting, or this time you're dead.*

* * *

"They must mean Len's painting," Gretchen said to no one in particular from her seat on the front-porch step. Her shock had meted out to a daze, but her fear stayed strong. "And they're willing to kill me for it."

Colm spoke from behind her to the few crew members peering in the windows. "Fellas, and Wendy, head back to the trailers for now. We're not done here, so don't go packing up yet. Stand by."

"Not done?" Gretchen gawked at him after he ushered the crew away. "Did you get a good look inside before the sheriff shut the door on us? They put holes in my walls. They thought I was hiding a painting behind them. Even if I had the painting, I wouldn't think to hide it there. Who *does* that?"

"Someone with something to hide, I suppose." Colm sat down beside her on the porch steps. "Maybe someone who's come from a world where secret hiding places are a must."

Gretchen sat in silence as the face of an old man appeared in her mind's eye. His stories echoed through her head as she recalled his tales from a world of unrest and fear, where secret hiding places were the norm in his homeland of Germany.

"Len," she answered quietly. "Len knew all

about hiding places, for all his valuables, including himself. Maybe he thinks his stolen painting is here, and he came looking for it. Maybe after it was stolen, he had some sort of flashback."

Colm scoffed, "I don't think the old man has the strength to bang through walls."

"You saw him with the crowbar, right? You even said he seemed touched with dementia. I don't know if it's that, but he is old. I think his memories from the war are coming back and he thinks they're real again. He's been through so much. If he thought someone was coming for him again, he might very well have enough strength to break through plaster to get the one thing he escaped with, so he could escape again."

"Was that the first time you noticed him behaving this way?"

"He's always spoken a lot of Germany, but only recently as though he was still there. I just wanted to believe he was reminiscing, not actually thinking the war was still happening. I guess I've been in denial about him getting old. Then he told me he was leaving me his painting, and there was no more denying it."

"I'd say he put you in danger the moment he did that."

The door behind them opened, jolting them to their feet. Sheriff Matthews stepped out with the previous island sheriff, now a detective on the mainland, Wesley Grant, and his forensics investigator wife, Lydia. Under any other circumstances Gretchen would have enjoyed catching up with them and hearing about the dynamic duo's cases. It was an old skeleton found on Stepping Stones Island a couple years ago that brought Lydia into Wesley's life. She'd put a smile back on Wesley's face, and the baby she looked to be expecting was evidence they were about to become a new kind of team.

But something about death threats took precedence, and judging by their somber faces, they understood.

"Looks like someone wanted you out of the house real bad last night," Wesley said to Gretchen as he closed the door behind him. "I wish I'd come over to the island earlier. I might have been able to put a stop to that demolition party before they destroyed everything in their path."

"Wesley," Lydia chided her husband, glancing at Gretchen. "Not so callous with your words, please."

"You're right, dear. Sorry, Gretchen. Any idea what painting they're looking for?"

Gretchen hated even to insinuate Len had a part in this disaster, but Colm jumped in and relayed all she'd told him. Sheriff Matthews said,

"I've had no leads with the painting and Len's been keeping to himself. Honestly, I thought he took the painting down at the restaurant when a few people voiced their displeasure about him leaving it to Gretchen. I can only assume they thought you already had it."

"So you think one of the islanders did this?" Gretchen asked.

"Can't say at this point, but we'll be processing the house today to look for any evidence that might give us a lead."

"If it is an islander, then that means one of my own tried to kill me."

"Or just found a way to get you out of the house. They may also be the one who left you at the clinic."

"You'll have to excuse me, but I'm not feeling the love. Especially since now I'm out of a home." Gretchen stood up. "Sheriff, if it's all right with you, I'd like to go see Len."

"Go ahead. I'll be over to chat with him later. And, Gretchen, I'm sorry about all this. It will be a sad day on Stepping Stones if one of our own is responsible."

Gretchen took the path to the barn for her car. Then she realized Colm walked beside her. "You might as well get your crew packed up. No sense in hanging around here anymore."

He halted and reached for her forearm to stop her. "I don't believe what I'm hearing."

"Then I'll say it again for you. Go home, Colm." She pulled her arm out of his grasp and walked on.

"Last night, not even a near-death incident would stop you. What happened? What's changed?"

"I'm just finally accepting that my ideas of a new life were far-fetched. It's time to go back to my old life and strap my apron back on."

"I can't accept this, Goldie," Colm called from behind. "I won't. Not without a fight."

Gretchen kept walking. She had no fight left in her.

"Give me the keys. Going forward I'm not leaving your side."

"I said go home."

"You're plum knackered right now and not thinking clearly. Or did you forget someone out there wants you dead? Now give me the keys."

"Some might say the Underground Küchen, or *kitchen* in English, got its name because it was built into the side of a cliff and is half-underground," Gretchen explained.

"Some? What would you say?" Colm asked.

"Len opened it when he escaped to the island after WWII. I think he named it for what it was." She flashed a smile. "It's just like my B&B sign for The Morning Glory. They are our covert-operation names for freedom."

"Glad to see your smile back in place."

The beautiful expression flitted away with the sea breeze whipping about them. She looked ahead as they approached the boardwalk.

"Were many people living here when Len came?" Colm asked as they walked past a long pier jutting out into the ocean from the boardwalk. Ornate lanterns lined the wooden walkway with benches beneath them.

"There were a few. The winters are long and difficult. It takes strong stock to make it here."

"Explains the strength I see in you. I recognized your *neart istigh* the moment I met you."

"What is that?"

"It's Irish for 'inner strength,' and you have it."

She shook her head. "It's not my strength you see. It belongs to Jesus. I would still be waiting tables here and taking my directions from Billy without Him. It was when I fully and truly understood that He bought my freedom that I knew He would also give me the strength to leave. In truth, I'm actually pretty weak."

"Because you think you allowed someone to hurt you? You didn't. That's part of the power an abuser has over his victim. It's like…"

"Puppet strings," she answered for him.

Colm nodded. "Yes. And I agree about the wonderful power of the Lord, but give yourself some credit, too. You took the first step and cut those strings. That took real *neart istigh*."

She led him in thoughtful silence past many storefronts running down one side of the boardwalk, with a restaurant at each end. Clothing, groceries and fishing equipment filled the stores' display windows.

"It would seem the shelves are well stocked," Colm said. "I'm surprised the islanders aren't jumping at having tourists on the island to shop at the stores."

"I had thought the same thing, but no. They're just as happy to keep their patrons local."

"Well, business can't be too good. Where is everyone? The boardwalk's empty."

"It's lunchtime. They're all inside my mom's restaurant. It's where everyone hangs out."

"Including Len?"

"Always Len. He lives in the house on the cliff, right above the restaurant. There's a secret staircase that's not really a secret because everyone knows about it, that runs up the back of the restaurant to his home. He comes and goes all day long and eats every meal at his table there."

"Secret staircase, huh? Sounds like he thought of everything after he escaped from Germany.

But if all he brought with him from his homeland was a painting, what would he need with secret hideaways and staircases? Unless he had other secrets to protect."

"Don't go all spy-like on me, Mr. Bond. The man risked everything and gave up his family to come here."

"So he came alone?"

"Not exactly. He came with two other men, another German man and a French man, who were also on the run. The restaurant on the other end of the boardwalk was owned by Frank Thibodaux, the French one."

"Was?"

"Len is the last remaining patriarch of the three."

"The last one to guard their secrets."

"Oh, stop," Gretchen said as they stepped up to the restaurant's entrance. "This isn't CIA's Most Wanted. This is tiny, little Stepping Stones Island." She reached for the glass door.

Colm stopped her from opening it. "A tiny, little island two and a half hours off the coast of America where three European men chose to live in secret. Think about it, Goldie. Who has the most to lose if tourists start showing up here? If Len is hiding secrets, it's not the shop owners. It's him."

"So you don't think this has something to

do with his getting old and maybe suffering from dementia?"

"It's just another possibility, but if Len is involved then that means he tried to kill you at least three times, and all three attempts were skilled and calculated. Not the work of a man going senile." Colm studied her pale face, her eyes sad. It wasn't the look he was hoping for. "You're not going to fight against him, are you?"

"It's Len Smith. I could never fight him."

"Smith. If that's even his real name. What was it before he went into hiding?"

Gretchen bit her lower lip. After a moment of hesitancy, she said, "I don't know. I never questioned it. Why would I?"

"Well, after three attempts on your life, you need to start."

"I'm sure you're wrong about Len. I really don't think he's behind the attacks."

"You'd be surprised what people will do if pushed far enough." He swung the door wide. "After you."

"Oh, great, make me go first into the fox den."

"You're just as cunning as any of them, love. Chin up." Colm smiled when her dainty chin raised a notch. "Atta girl."

Once he entered behind her, though, he saw she would need a little more pluck to handle this crowd. The place was filled with muted faces staring at her. Had coming here been a bad idea?

"Greetings," Colm said into the silence. "I'm Colm McCrae, host of *Rescue to Restoration*. Gretchen and I are here to see—"

"Oh, Gretchen, your face." A woman with long golden-red hair rushed from a table to Gretchen's side. She used her hands to say something in sign language, and Colm realized she was deaf. "Owen told me about your injury, but seeing you like this hurts so much more."

"Colm, this is Miriam, Sheriff Matthews's wife."

Colm nodded, but Miriam didn't pay him a lick of attention. No one in the room did, for that matter. Each person who now approached them only pushed him out of the picture.

Well, that was a first. Colm cracked a smile. No one cared that they had a television personality in their midst. And he couldn't lie. He liked it.

He especially liked seeing how they all doted on Gretchen. These were the people she'd told him loved her, and by the affection he was witnessing, she had been correct. He found it hard to believe any of these people would hurt her. Some of them looked as if they wanted to hurt Billy Baker, though.

A bristly fisherman walked up to Colm and

even though he came to his chin, the short man managed to look him in the eyes. "I thought you were Irish. You don't sound very Irish. Are you a phony?"

Colm took in the crowd, who suddenly quieted to hear the answer. "I'm not a phony, I can tell you that. Let's just say we all have things we'd like to forget. Where I come from is one of mine. My director thinks otherwise and requires me to use my native tongue on camera. End of story."

A few shrugs told him some were content with his explanation. Gretchen's tilted head showed she was unsure. She still didn't trust him completely, and there really was no time for her to learn to. Perhaps when she was safe, they could... They could what? Build a different kind of house, one that would give them a future together?

Colm nearly scoffed out loud. He felt the blood rush to his head and knew his fair Irish complexion had to be beet red. What was this young colleen doing to him? She had him running circles around her, trying to keep her safe, all while trying to make her smile. For what? So he could turn into a flustered young buck? Perhaps he was the one going mad around here, not Len.

Gretchen said to the people around her, "We came to see Len. Is he here?"

The crowd looked around until someone spoke up. "Nope. In fact, come to think of it, I haven't seen him all day. Anyone else?"

No one chimed in. Just a bunch of shaking heads and widening eyes as it dawned on all of them that the town's elder hadn't shown his face to anyone all day. A few men rushed to the back swinging doors, but Gretchen beat them there.

Colm raced after her, and over the heads of the men in front of him, he saw her lead the way up a back stairwell that looked to be a lit cavern. She took the steps two at a time, and Colm had all he could do not to climb over the old men to get to her.

"Gretchen!" he called to her, but her steps didn't slow. She reached the top stair and froze. Colm couldn't see what she saw, but her whimper had him elbowing past the men. "Goldie, what is it?"

The men allowed him to pass, and he stepped up to a landing. Another staircase led up to a door that must lead into Len's house, but the crumpled man lying at the foot of the stairs halted any more assumptions.

"Len." Gretchen ran to his side.

"Goldie, don't touch him. His neck could be broken."

"I know," she replied. Her fingers gently felt for a pulse. "He's alive." Her shoulders slumped in a sigh. "Someone call 911. Tell them Len fell down the stairs."

Two of the men ran back downstairs as Colm knelt on the other side of Len. He took in the bruised face with distinct markings that had nothing to do with a fall. "I hate to tell you this, Goldie, but Len didn't fall."

She raised her face to him. "How do you know?"

"I'd know a five-finger face-pummel any day of the week. Len Smith has been through a belting and left here to make it look like he fell."

"Who would do such a thing to a man in his nineties?"

"Someone who wanted to make sure his secrets stayed a secret," he said, and Gretchen shot him a quick glance. "Or someone who found out his secrets."

She leaned over the man. "Len, it's me, Gretchen. I'm right beside you. We're going to get you to a hospital."

"Gret…mmmm…Gret," Len mumbled from a faraway place of consciousness.

Gretchen inhaled in a rush of surprise. "Yes, it's me. I'm here, Len. We're all here. We're getting you help, but we need you to fight. Do you hear me?"

His eyes flashed wide on a sharp inhale. "Gretch…Gretchen."

She leaned closer to the man as his hand reached for her. "Can you tell us what happened?"

"Forgive me," Len rasped out.

"Forgive you for what?"

"Attic. Attic. So sorry. They're coming for—" Len made an awful breathing sound.

"Who's coming? Wait!" she said when Doctor Schaffer appeared at her side. Colm came up behind her to pull her away so the doctor could do his work. "I need to know what he's talking about."

"He's probably not making a wee bit of sense," Colm said, trying to comfort her. "Don't pay any mind to it."

"How can I not? He mentioned the attic! What is he saying? He's apologizing. What did he… do?"

Gretchen took a step back into Colm's arms. He felt her body start to tremble.

"He did it, didn't he?" she said, turning her face into Colm's neck. "That's what he wants my forgiveness for. He doused the attic with turpentine. Len's the one who nearly killed me."

Colm tightened his hold on her just as her knees gave out.

TEN

"We're home," Colm said as he pulled Gretchen's car into the long driveway. The words sounded grand on his lips as it had been so long since he had referenced any place as home.

He expected Gretchen to set him straight, but a glance to his right showed she hadn't heard him at all. It was just as well, but he would have rather his words zapped her out of this listless state that left her like a piece of driftwood.

"You know you can't take what Len said to heart. You know his mind on a good day was confused."

"Do you think we can get into my house yet?" Her lack of response told him she wasn't ready to talk about it. "I have to start making phone calls."

"For what?"

"Cancellations. I can't have people showing up here in three weeks."

Colm put the car into Park. "I'll agree with

you about the three weeks, but don't cancel permanently."

"Lydia's coming out of the house," Gretchen announced and jumped from the car.

Colm followed her to the front door and heard Lydia say, "Gretchen, I need to talk with you." She eyed Colm. "Privately."

Colm didn't move. He wanted to be kept abreast of the situation, and he definitely wasn't up for leaving Gretchen's side anytime soon, even if she believed Len was behind it all. "I don't think Gretchen should be alone until we know for certain the person doing this is behind bars. But I understand, Gretchen, if you'd rather I wait on the porch—"

"No," she cut him off.

Colm started to debate but sighed and gave in. "All right, if that's what you want. I'll be at my trailer."

"No, I mean I don't want you to leave. And I don't want you on the porch." She gazed at the place beside her and barely raised her eyes when she said, "I want you right here."

Air whooshed from his lungs. "Are you certain, love?" Colm stepped up next to her. He turned her face so she would look him straight in the eye. All he saw was fear staring back at him. "You're not certain."

He saw that her inner strength warred with

her inner struggle: to depend on another person when she'd promised herself to stand on her own.

"You're not breaking any pact you made with yourself," he assured her. "Consider me support while you face some pretty scary, very abnormal, I might add, challenges. Nothing more."

A slight smile crossed her pretty lips. As her battle dissipated, her dainty shoulders relaxed and welcomed his hand as he grasped hers, reassuring her of his presence while she faced these nightmares. He rubbed gently. Deep down he knew his fingers memorized the feel of her for the day she shrugged him off for good. He would have to be a complete fool if he thought the day wouldn't come.

"Okay, Lydia, what did you find?" Gretchen asked the forensic scientist, her voice not sounding too eager for the news that could confirm her worst nightmare: that Len Smith did try to kill her.

Lydia looked around to scan the foyer to make sure they were alone. She faced them again. "Out of curiosity, how well do you know the painter Ethan?"

Gretchen said, "He's very kind."

At the same time, Colm said, "Not too well."

At Lydia's arched eyebrows, he continued,

"Not at all really. He's new to our crew. Came highly recommended, though. Why?"

"Wesley did a background check on every one of the crew." She paused and looked at Colm.

"And his past is as colorful as mine? Is that what you're trying to say?"

"No, actually, his is perfect. Not even a speeding ticket."

"And that worries you? Maybe he's just a real good guy who's never been in any trouble."

She bounced her head side to side as though she weighed his response. "Possibly, but it's so clean that it almost seems faked." She turned and picked up a black hard-shell case. "And I also found this." She opened the case and removed a plastic bag with something inside. "I believe it's the paintbrush used to leave the message. Tests will need to be run to match the paint, and the prints I lifted from it will need to be processed."

"Where did you find it?" Gretchen asked.

"In Ethan's bucket upstairs in one of the bedrooms. Which reminds me, his equipment is not well maintained. You say he comes with high recommendations, but what kind of painter doesn't clean his brushes?" She held up the bag. Red paint was hardened to the bristles. "This wasn't the only ruined brush."

"So he doesn't clean his brushes." Gretchen

frowned. "There's no crime in that. And even if you find his prints on the brush, which I'm sure you will because it's his, that doesn't mean Ethan is guilty of anything. Len pretty much confessed to being the one to hurt me. You can keep searching for evidence, but nothing trumps a confession."

"He confessed? Does Sheriff Matthews know?"

"Not yet. He wasn't there when Len spoke to me."

Lydia placed the brush back into her case. "All right, if you think Ethan is clean, even if his brushes aren't, I'll back off. He's in the attic with Wesley now. Wesley had a few questions for him, and being pregnant I stayed out of there."

Colm bypassed them and headed for the stairs. "You stay out, too, Gretchen. We don't need a repeat asthma attack."

One flight up, then to the attic stairs, Colm found Ethan and Detective Grant in a silent standoff.

"Why do I smell something rotten up here that isn't the turpentine?" Colm asked.

Detective Grant barely moved. "My wife is concerned your painter isn't really a painter. I was just asking him how he planned to clean up the turpentine, and he doesn't seem to have a clue. My deductive skills say he's been lying to you. Perhaps it was just to obtain a job. Or perhaps it was something a little more premeditated. Either way, he's coming with me to speak with Sheriff Matthews. He's sure to have his own questions for Mr. Hunt, if that's even your name. Let's go find out."

Ethan's eyes sent sharp daggers at Detective Grant when the man grabbed his arm and pushed him to move. "You're making a big mistake." He passed Colm, sharing some of those daggers with him.

The two men stepped downstairs, and Colm could hear Gretchen questioning Detective Grant as they passed to the front door.

"Where are you taking Ethan?" she asked. "It was Len who hurt me. Ethan's been a comfort to me."

Colm stood at the top of the staircase, listening to her high esteem for Ethan, and all he could wonder was if her feelings for the man ran deeper than friendship.

He wondered what he would do if Gretchen had romantic feelings for Ethan. What would he say? But then, what could he say? If Ethan's background check was accurate, then he was exactly the type of man Gretchen deserved. An all-around nice fella. He'd never even had a speeding ticket.

ELEVEN

Gretchen's planner lay open on her bed, and she had already dialed the first guest's phone number on her phone. All she had to do was hit Call. One button to begin the cancellation process…and end her dreams forever.

She thought back to the interview three months ago that had set her plans in motion and started the flood of reservations.

After she'd taken Troy and his cameraman for a walk down the snowy boardwalk, she'd sat down with him in front of the fireplace at the restaurant and gave the viewers a warm window into her world. A fire glowed behind them in the huge hearth. She hadn't known how vibrant the interview had been until the preview aired. She'd worn a blue woolen sweater that matched her eyes but hadn't realized when she'd chosen it that it would also pull the colors from the painting above the fireplace.

Troy had asked all the right questions about

heritage and history. He'd wanted her to share all she knew about the first inhabitants of the island, who happened to be pilfering pirates. He'd portrayed amazement on the screen when she told him about a sunken ship left over from the pirate days still off the island's coast. He'd also asked her to relay some of the tales she grew up hearing from the elders on the island and how they came to find such a gem…and how they kept it a secret for so long.

A secret.

The word affected her differently now. She had laughed it off with Troy, saying they didn't intend to keep it a secret. The island was just so far from the mainland that no one went out that far unless they were invited. It was one of those places that someone had to tell you about.

Gretchen remembered smiling at the camera and leaning in. She told the viewers, "Consider yourselves told and invited." She leaned back and shook Troy's hand to begin a great partnership with him and his crew. Then the camera pulled away from them and lifted to the painting above as music ended the interview session and the screen blackened before going to a commercial.

Gretchen jumped from her bedside, her throat dry in an instant on a sharp intake of air.

Len's painting had been aired for the world to see.

Gretchen paced her floor wondering if it had been that interview that incited the danger. Had it scared Len into thinking someone would come for it? Did it make him so angry with her that he lashed out and tried to kill her? Had the airing of the interview made him paranoid that someone from his past would come looking for it, *or him*, on his island?

His *secret* island.

The screech of a power tool wrenched through her empty house. Gretchen jolted at the sound, confused as to why someone ran it. The crew was supposed to be packing up to leave the island. The renovation wouldn't be continuing as planned.

So, then, who was in her house?

She dropped the phone to her bed and went to the door. Her hand rested on the doorknob, but before she turned it she noticed the crowbar leaning against the wall. It had been put there after Len visited that first day the crew arrived. When she saw him holding it, she had thought it humorous to think an old man in his nineties would be able to hurt anyone.

"I won't make that mistake again," she said and grabbed hold of the heavy, cold bar. She opened her bedroom door with the crowbar raised for protection.

The power tool echoed off the walls of the immense hall and foyer. She followed the sound to the railing and looked down to where it came from.

Colm knelt down at the foot of the stairs, cutting away the broken boards where she'd fallen through.

Calling down to him would be useless over the noise. She also didn't want to startle him and make him slip with the saw. Gretchen decided to wait a few minutes until he put the tool down. She walked to the top of the stairs and sat down, planning to ask him just what he was up to, when the saw stopped. Except when the last echoing screech of the power tool filled her house, it was replaced by a pleasant whistling tune coming from Colm's lips.

Instead of alerting him to her presence, Gretchen sat still and listened…and watched. For two years she had seen this handsome television host crack jokes and melt hearts with his smiling eyes. Since she met him two weeks ago, she'd learned that the host wasn't who he appeared to be and that he came from a life of street fighting and basic survival. But knowing this didn't tell her who he really was, either.

Colm whipped out a tape measure and pencil,

still hunched over, then made quick work of preparing the floor for new boards.

She almost laughed aloud. The house was filled with holes in the walls all around her, and here he was whistling away as content as could be with the one in front of him.

He also looked as though he knew exactly what he was doing.

He wasn't a fraud at all.

Colm's whimsical Irish melody came to an abrupt halt, and Gretchen looked from his hands to his face staring up at her.

"When did you get there?" he asked. He smiled broadly...which did funny things to her belly.

"A few minutes ago." She shrugged and played with the crowbar still in her hands. "I didn't want to disturb you. You seemed very involved in your work. I don't think I've ever seen you so...happy. What song were you whistling?"

"Something my da would whistle when he was in his woodshop." Colm laughed and said, "I never knew the song had words until I was much older. I found out there was a reason he whistled it and never sang it."

Gretchen laughed, too. "Not appropriate for young ears?"

"Hardly." Colm made a mark on the floor

with his pencil and grabbed his manual saw to cut a hanging piece. "A penny?"

Gretchen's smile relaxed. She tilted her head. "I was just thinking that I finally figured out who you are."

He put the saw back into his bucket. "Who I am? I'm Colm McCrae. That's nothing new."

"No. Before I met you, I only knew you as the funny-talking TV personality. Okay, and the cute one, too. But then you came here, and I saw a side of you that, well, I'll be honest, scared me."

The shine in his eyes dimmed. "I would never hurt you, Gretchen. You have nothing to be afraid of."

"I know. That's what I'm trying to say. Your TV personality isn't who you are. Your past as a street fighter doesn't define you, either. Sitting here, watching you, I finally see."

He raised one eyebrow with a smirk. "I'm almost afraid to hear this."

Gretchen smiled down at him. "Don't be. It's good. Real good. You're a carpenter, Colm."

His smirk evaporated in an instant. He shook his head a few times before he said, "Nay. My da was a carpenter. I just play one on the telly."

Gretchen frowned at his denial of her observation. But she also knew he'd had a lifetime of believing the worst of himself. Colm's dysfunctional past told her that a declaration of his true identity wasn't going to change his self-image instantly. No, it would take more than words for him to believe.

She reached over and caressed the spindle of the original ornate railing that ran along the upstairs balcony. It had once continued down the staircase, sweeping out at the bottom. "You know, the rest of this railing is out back in the barn. It's in pretty rough shape. I had planned on buying new, figuring it would be cheaper and easier to replace it rather than restoring the original."

"Seriously? You have the rest of the railing?"

"Yeah. Do you think it's worth restoring? Or should I just replace it?"

Colm scanned the railing above him. "I'd have to take a look at it, but I might be able to bring it back to its original beauty. I'd love to try."

Gretchen beamed at him. "See what I mean? You're a true carpenter. Face it, Colm."

"Or what? You'll knock me out with that crowbar?" He skeptically eyed the bar in her hand.

Gretchen nearly forgot she still held it. "When I heard the saw, I grabbed it in case…well, in case there was an unfriendly person out here."

"Good. Glad to see you're taking this seriously. But since you brought it out, bring it down here so I can lift out the broken boards."

Gretchen stood to descend the stairs. At the bottom, Colm took the crowbar and gave a quick pull on a board. It came out clean. He moved on to another board.

"That one isn't broken," she said. "Why are you taking it?"

"It's uneven with the floor. I figured since I was replacing the cut boards, I would replace this one, too. I wouldn't want your guests tripping over it."

Gretchen shook her head. "The Morning Glory won't be opening its doors. But I know what you mean about these old floorboards. When I was trapped in the attic I tried to move a chest over to the window so I could reach to open it. But the chest hit a raised floorboard and fell over."

"I'm so sorry you had to go through that."

"I'm sorrier Len put me through it. If I had known when I saw him carrying this crowbar out of the attic that he meant to hurt me, I would have—" Gretchen stopped, an odd look on her face.

"What? You would have what?" Colm attempted to pull her back to the conversation. "Gretchen?"

"May I see that crowbar for a second?"

Colm passed it over to her. "What are you thinking, Goldie?"

"I'm not sure. Seeing you lift the boards gave me an idea. What would Len need this for if all he planned to do was pour turpentine on the floor? Come on." She picked up her steps on the stairs with Colm right behind her.

"Maybe he wasn't up there putting something on my floor," she said. "Maybe he was up there putting something *in* my floor."

The attic still held a trace of the licorice and piney fumes, but for the most part the turpentine spill had been cleaned up, thanks to Sly. The man had a wealth of knowledge and was always quick to help where he was needed. After Ethan had been carted away the day before, Colm was glad to have his old friend to fall back on, especially since Colm planned to continue this restoration whether Gretchen still believed in her dreams or not. He would believe enough for her.

"The uneven board was right in here." Gretchen led the way into the attic room. The room stood empty except for a chest pushed up against a side wall. A broken window was all that remained of the evidence of Gretchen's torture.

Colm's stomach twisted when he thought of

her laboring for air, the window above blocking her.

"Someone moved the chest to the wall, I think. I don't remember pushing it that far. It was dark, but I'm pretty sure it had been situated right in the middle of the room." She moved to the center. "Right here, I think."

Colm joined her search for a floorboard that looked higher than the others. When she bent to touch the floor with her bare hands, he told her to stop. "There still could be traces of the turpentine. I don't want it on your hands."

"I hope there are no traces left." She straightened back up. "This place could go up like a torch. Thank the Lord it hadn't already."

Colm smiled. "So you aren't ready to let the old house go after all. There's hope for you still." He knelt to take over and quickly found the board she had bumped. "I think I found it." He pulled at the board's edge, but it didn't budge.

"Try the crowbar to lift it like you did to the board downstairs." She handed him the piece of steel and stepped back.

Colm inserted the flat wedged end down the side of the board. He cranked the bar down, but it didn't go far.

Gretchen circled around him. "Wait, I think you should try from this end. See how these boards end at the same place? It's as though they were all cut at the same length, unlike the rest of the wood boards that vary in length and starting point."

Colm changed positions and inserted the tool where she specified. One crank and up popped not one board, but eight.

Colm halted in surprise, the gap only a few inches up from the floor. "It's a trapdoor." He shot a look up at Gretchen. Her eyes were full of shock and wonder.

"Go ahead, Colm. Open it. Don't keep me waiting." Her impatience mimicked exuberance, but he couldn't fault her. He felt the same way.

Reaching his fingers under the lifted edge, Colm brought the boards to their straight-up position, and there, in a five-by-five wooden compartment, lay something shaped like a rectangle and wrapped in brown paper.

"Three guesses?" he asked, stepping back for her to do the honors. "Or should we just tear into it?"

"Tear." Gretchen knelt and lifted the rectangle out of its hiding place. Her fingers dug in at the corners. Someone listening would have thought it was Christmas morning with all the paper tearing and rejoicing cries that followed, Colm thought.

He sat beside her and brought the painting onto both their laps.

A European country scene with a stone wall and a path filled the piece of art. A lone figure, a painter judging by the artistic tools slung on his back, walked along under bright blue skies with two trees behind him. Leaves of assorted fall colors lay on the ground around the figure. The man was familiar-looking with his yellow-brimmed hat.

"Colm, do you know what this means?" Gretchen turned to him with tears filling her eyes.

"Um…Len had a van Gogh hanging on your restaurant wall all these years?"

"No, it means… Wait, what? This is a van Gogh?"

"Well, I'm far from an art scholar, but I've seen enough of van Gogh's self-portraits to recognize him out for a stroll."

Gretchen's mouth fell wide. "Do you think it's a reproduction?"

"Why would Len go to such great lengths to hide it here in your house if it were?"

"True, but I still can't believe this. A van Gogh?" Seconds elapsed into minutes as she processed the find. "The painting had hung over the fireplace for so long, it became almost invisible to us. None of us thought anything of it. But when the show aired the interview, it showed the painting on the wall for anyone watching to see.

Len must have known someone would recognize it. He hid it because he wanted to protect it. I think we should put it back. At least until we know what's going on and who's after it… enough to try to kill me. I hope this means it wasn't Len after all."

"Regardless of whether he set up the attacks, Len still put you in danger by hiding this here. Honestly, Gretchen, I'd rather see you live than protect a piece of canvas."

"He must have had his reasons, or his fear of losing it caused him not to think clearly until it was too late. Even so, I don't hold anything against him. I want to believe that he was apologizing for stashing this here, not for dousing the place. Don't be mad at him. Please."

"For you, Goldie, I won't be. And I'll put this back. Mum's the word. But this also means the crew's not going anywhere." Colm laid the painting back in its hiding place and concealed it by lowering the door over it.

"Colm, I can't pay for the extra repairs. It's over."

"I didn't say anything about you paying. I've been saving some money for my ma. I had this crazy idea that I could buy her freedom."

Gretchen tilted her head and frowned. "I'm sorry to say this, but it would take more than money to break the hold your stepfather has over her."

"I guess I've always known that, but I still saved the money in hopes that maybe I could show her she didn't need him to take care of her."

"Then I definitely can't take your money when you're saving it for such a noble cause."

"A lost cause. I have to accept that Gil Griffin's chains are permanent. It won't matter how much money I save, Ma will never leave him."

"I'll pray for her. Every day."

"Thank you. And I'll use what I have to cover the costs here and appease Troy."

"No, Colm, I can't ask you to do that."

"You didn't, but it would be all right if you did, you know. There's nothing wrong with asking for help. It doesn't make you weak. God tells us that those who trust in themselves are fools, but those who walk in wisdom are kept safe. Let me keep you safe, Goldie. By making sure you have a home."

Colm turned his body until he faced her, and his knee brushed against hers. He reached out to stroke her cheek. "Please, let me help you."

The struggle for her independence showed on her face. Colm traced the lines of worry near her eyes with his thumb. She squeezed her eyes shut, then opened them before she visibly relaxed under his touch.

He turned her face to his. "You're so brave. You know that, right?"

She shrugged slightly.

"Aye. You are. Since the day I met you, you wore the look of determination I always wished to see in my ma."

"Oh, Colm, I'm so sorry she has to live like that. That you had to live like that, too."

"Not to worry about me. It's all grand now. Even more so since I came to your island."

"How's that?"

"Something Sheriff Matthews said when I was at the department has really made things clear. My mother was protecting me when I had wanted to protect her. She sent me away when all I wanted was to help her. At the time it hurt, but I see now she feared I would become another bully like Gil. And she was right in her thinking. I would have and even did."

"No," Gretchen argued. "I told you that's not who you are." She put her hand over his. "You're gentle. You're hardworking." She smiled. "You're funny."

Colm dropped his gaze to her lips so close to his. Her smile trembled. "Is that all?" he whispered.

She shook her head. "You're caring and protective and…beautiful." Her gaze drifted to his lips. A puff of air escaped hers. Colm hoped the battle within her was coming to an end.

"Gretchen," Colm whispered, "you've turned me inside out. The only way I'm right again is to be near you. You give me so much hope, *a chara, a stór, a ghrá. A chuisle mo chroí.*"

"What does that mean?"

"My friend, my treasure, my love. You are the pulse of my heart."

"Oh, Colm, I don't think we—"

"Wait. Don't push me away. Not yet. Let me kiss you. Please."

Moments passed. If no response came from her lips, he would have to let her go. He wouldn't push her to make a decision she would regret.

No answer came.

"Not to worry, love," he assured her and pulled back, but before he departed a mere inch from her, Gretchen pressed in, reaching around the back of his head and pulling him in to meet her lips.

The shock of her movements vanished in an instant as Colm met her and took control of the kiss. This had not been an easy decision for her, and Colm wouldn't take it for granted.

The touch of her sweet lips made him think he could believe all those wonderful things she said about him. She was a smart woman and would never bestow such a precious gift on an undeserving street fighter. No, Gretchen would offer such a gift of letting down her barriers only for someone she loved.

Loved.

Colm deepened the kiss at this revelation. Could it be? Could the amazingly beautiful and intelligent Gretchen Bauer love him? A lowlife from the slums of Dublin?

Colm was so bowled over at the thought that he missed the pressure on his chest. He mistook the strain for the rapid beating of his heart, but another push tore him from Gretchen's lips and sent him a foot back. Her barriers were reerected like a stone-cold wall between them. Colm could see the fear in her eyes.

"I would never harm you. Please tell me you know this," he pleaded as he reached for her hands.

Gretchen quickly stood. "This won't happen again. I'm sorry."

Colm looked up at her. "You have nothing to be sorry for."

"I wasn't apologizing to you. I was apologizing to myself. You've made a promise to yourself not to fight. Well, I've also made one. There's no place for you in my life. I'm on my own." She made tracks to the door and rushed down the stairs.

Colm jumped to his feet and followed her down the attic stairs. At the hall she was making her way down the grand staircase.

"Gretchen, can we talk about this?" he called out as she reached the first floor and opened the front door.

Sheriff Matthews stood on the other side, bringing her to a halt. "Gretchen, I need to speak with you."

Colm made his way down the stairs to hear what news the lawman brought. Was Gretchen in more danger? He came up beside her and waited to hear what the sheriff had to say.

The man looked from Gretchen to him and said, "Sorry, Colm, but I need to speak with her alone."

When Lydia had said this the day before, Gretchen had requested he stay.

She didn't this time.

Colm left her side and passed through the door. He nodded at Sheriff Matthews as he went by. "That's all right. That's the way she likes things. Alone."

TWELVE

"We need your secrecy on a matter that has landed on the shores of Stepping Stones and involves someone on the crew…and now involves all of us," Sheriff Matthews stated when he was sure the house stood empty, minus the two of them.

"More secrets?" Gretchen sighed. "I'm so tired of them."

"I understand your hesitation, and typically I would never ask, but I don't believe Len is the one responsible for hurting you, which means you're still in danger."

Gretchen walked to the stairs and took the first step for a seat. Owen joined her. "I had thought he was admitting to hurting me. He'd apologized for the attic, and I believed the worst of him." Tears filled her eyes, but she stopped them before they spilled out. "But the turpentine wasn't what he was talking about. He was apologizing because he hid his most valuable possession in my attic. His painting." She looked at the ceiling.

Owen's eyes widened. "The painting's here? Right now?"

She nodded. "Nobody stole it. I'm thinking Len got scared that someone would come for it, and he must have thought it would be safe with me and hid it in a hiding place that I didn't even know existed." She looked at Owen and sighed. "And it's all my fault. He was attacked by someone who wanted it because I alerted the world to its existence. I might as well have handwritten the invite."

"How do you figure?"

"Remember when Troy came to the island to interview me? After I showed him around the island and this house, I took him back to the restaurant and we sat in front of the fireplace. The last screen shot was of the painting hanging above us. So you see, I did this. Anyone could have seen that clip and come looking for it. Even try to kill for it."

"There's more to the story, Gretchen. More that I just recently found out myself."

"What is it?"

"This is where I need your secrecy. I shouldn't be even telling you. I'm sure I'm breaking a federal law, but we decided you could aid us in narrowing down the suspects who are after this painting."

"Aid you? And what do you mean by *federal*?"

"Can you promise you'll keep it quiet? It could mean putting lives at risk if you let anything slip."

"I understand."

"Your aid could put a stop to the crimes right here and for good."

"Crimes? As in plural? You mean this isn't the first?"

He shook his head. "And won't be the last unless they are caught."

Someone was out there victimizing innocent people—including herself—for artwork? How could she say no? "What is it you need me to do?"

"Can I take this as your promise?"

Gretchen straightened up with an emphatic nod. "I will help catch whoever is trying to hurt people for their own gain. Where do we begin?"

"Hold up just a second." Owen grabbed the radio at his shoulder and pushed the button to speak. "Come on in. It's a go."

"Is that Wesley?"

The next second Ethan appeared above her, coming through the servants' quarters. He stopped at the top of the stairs and looked down at them.

Gretchen jumped to her feet. "Ethan, what are you doing here? You shouldn't be in the house. How much did you hear?"

"Enough." He took the first step down, his gait slow and deliberate. He came another few stairs and Gretchen eased back, nearly falling into the hole that Colm had yet to finish. "Enough to know you can be trusted," Ethan said as he reached the landing. Ethan put his hand out. "I'm Special Agent Ethan Hunt, undercover for the FBI. I'm sure you figured out by now that I'm not a painter." He flashed a genuine smile, but Gretchen couldn't make herself respond.

"Gretchen," Owen said, "this is the secret we need you to keep. If word gets out the production crew is being watched by the FBI, there could be a backlash we have yet to see the likes of."

"Worse than someone trying to kill me?"

"Ethan doesn't think anyone's been trying to kill you."

"Seriously?" Gretchen couldn't believe Owen's words.

Ethan explained, "If they wanted you dead, you'd be dead. I believe they just wanted you off the property so they could look around for the painting. I'm pretty sure whoever doused the place with turpentine to cause your asthma attack was also the one who rescued you and got you to the clinic."

"Really?" Gretchen was still incredulous.

"My point being, if it should slip that the FBI is onto someone in this crew for art theft, those setups will be carried through to the fullest extent."

Air rushed from Gretchen's lungs. "Meaning no more accidents, only death."

The two men didn't have to answer.

"I can't believe this," she mumbled before accepting Ethan's words. "So, how long has this been going on?"

"Right about the time Colm came on."

The air in her lungs rushed out. "You think Colm is behind this? But he was at the police station when I got locked in the attic. He couldn't have done it or rescued me."

"He could have an accomplice. Someone he trusts with his life."

"Sly."

Both men nodded, and Gretchen's heart rate sped up to the point she felt it pulsing through her head. It couldn't be Colm. He was a good man. She'd finally seen it. His past didn't define him anymore. He'd said he was a new creation in Christ. That Sly had introduced him to God and told him there was always another way.

"Another way," she mumbled.

"Another way for what?" Ethan asked.

"Nothing. It's nothing," she replied, but deep down she had to wonder if fencing art was Colm's other way of fighting back against a world that had cut him down so many times.

"He always wanted me to go to the clinic. Right from the first accident. The first day I met him, he said I shouldn't even be on the scene. It wasn't customary for the home owner to stay."

"I'm sure it made things easier in the past for them."

"Past? How many thefts have there been?"

"Thanks to you, it will be stopping at five."

"Five." A horrid thought popped into her head. "What about Len? Colm could never have beaten him up. I know this."

"How do you know it? Gretchen, Colm McCrae was a street fighter. His track record proves he could have done it…and has."

"But he says God has changed him. Come on, Owen, you know the transformation God can accomplish in our lives when we follow Him. I have to believe He did it for Colm, too."

"Why do you have to believe that?"

Because I kissed him, and I wanted to do it again. The words blared through her head. When she had leaned into him and forgot all her vows so easily, her actions scared her. To feel such strong emotions for another man, after she pledged never to feel that way again, proved she was weak.

She thought of how she had melted at his beautiful Irish words. Billy had never been so graceful with his words. Colm McCrae was the smoothest talker out there.

"Maybe I shouldn't be helping you," Gretchen said. "I may not be strong enough for this task."

"We think you are, or we wouldn't have asked," Ethan assured her. "Don't worry about messing things up. I'm going to return as painter, and you just continue as usual. I'll follow my suspicions where they lead, which reminds me, I'm sorry I left you the night you were locked in the attic. I caught Troy snooping around after hours and followed him until he went back to his trailer."

"Troy!" Gretchen exclaimed. "He's mean and selfish and only cares about money. Are you considering him?"

"Of course, we're considering all the crew members who have been at the reported theft locations. But as I said, the art started to disappear from people's homes when Colm came on the program. He has a mother he's trying to get over to the States."

"His savings fund," Gretchen remembered aloud. "He said he would use some of it to fix my house, so the crew could stay on and finish. He literally just told me about it upstairs when—"

"When what?" Ethan asked.

"When we found the painting together. Colm knows where it is. In fact, he said it was a van Gogh."

"Wow. They're going after a van Gogh this time, are they? And he knew what he was looking at?"

Gretchen nodded. The dread made her take her seat again on the bottom step.

Colm was guilty? No, she couldn't believe it.

Sheriff Matthews cleared his throat as he peered out the window. "Colm's coming. What should we do about the painting? Should we move it?"

"No," Ethan said. "Right now he's the only one besides Gretchen and Len who knows where it is. Len's at the hospital on the mainland. So if it goes missing, we know who took it."

Nausea rolled in Gretchen's stomach. She felt as if she was now the hated puppet master pulling the strings. Never would she have wanted to play this part.

Colm's booted footsteps hit the porch. Each beat jerked her shoulders.

"Get ready, Gretchen. It's showtime."

Sheriff Matthews opened the door before Colm could knock. "Colm, I'm glad you're here.

I brought back Ethan. We've checked him out and he's clean."

"Well, you can take him right back out with you. I don't want him anywhere near this site."

Ethan stepped up, his hands out to plead. "I'm sorry I exaggerated on my résumé, but please, I need this job. You don't understand. I have family struggling with health and finances. I did what I had to for them."

Colm clenched his jaw, and just as he began to shake his head, Gretchen stood up and spoke, even though each word caused her physical pain: "Colm, you said you would do whatever you could to get my house finished in time for the grand opening. The fact is, Ethan is the only painter you have on the crew. We need him. *I* need him. Please, let him stay."

Colm's face blanched. He took his eyes off her and looked at Ethan for a long moment. Back and forth his gaze passed between them until finally he nodded once. No happiness shined in his eyes. In fact, Gretchen thought his usual light dulled before her. He exited without a word, and for the first time in her life she knew what it felt like to control another human being.

"I'm going to be sick."

THIRTEEN

"Cut!" Troy jumped from his director's chair, red in the face. "McCrae! I won't be able to use any of this footage. It's boring! For nearly two weeks you've done nothing but work on this house, barely speaking to the camera. You only *play* a carpenter on TV. The viewers want to see your face, not your back. Put that cloth down and get back in front of the camera!"

Colm stood from giving the staircase railing a last swipe of polish. He could practically see his reflection in its shine. He stuffed the rag in his back jeans pocket and picked up his bucket of tools. He gave a quick look through the entry to the living room. The room stood empty of anyone so he looked above to Gretchen's closed bedroom door. He wanted to see her face when she saw the banister complete and finished for the first time. He wished his da could see it, as well. He wished his da could see everything his hands had touched these past two weeks.

I found who I am, Da, and Gretchen was right. I'm a carpenter just like you.

The house was nearing completion except for the servants' quarters. Those Gretchen could work on slowly as income from the guests replenished her coffers, even though Colm had a deep desire to stay on and continue what he'd started. The thought of staying on long after that entered his mind.

It flitted out just as fast.

Gretchen would never have it. She would never have him. These past two weeks had proven that.

He and his crew had worked day and night to finish her home. She herself had done the same, helping Ethan with painting as much as she could. Colm had worried about her asthma around the fumes, but she took the necessary precautions and showed no signs of labored breathing. If she had wheezed even once, he would have stepped in.

And done what? The woman was so independent. To even suggest she needed help offended her. And that was the reason any chance he had of sticking around after the restoration was bleak.

"Have you seen Gretchen?" he asked Troy as though he'd just noticed the man. "How about you, Nate?"

Nate brought his camera down from his shoulder. "She and Ethan are finishing up the side porch. Do you want me to go grab her?"

"Nay, I'll head out there and see how they're faring. I'm pretty much done in here. I'd say we do our walkthrough tonight. Then let's pack up and be on our way."

"You got it," Nate said.

"I say when we pack up," Troy interrupted. "I have some unfinished business here, and you have some footage to retake. You're not going anywhere until you get it right."

"I've given you all I got. The Sunday ferry arrives tomorrow, and I plan to be on it."

"Then you better tell the captain to sail east for Dublin. Maybe your alley is still available."

Colm heard Troy's threats, but now he knew they were empty. For two years the man threw them out like punches. One hit after another reminded Colm of his worthless past, the message that Colm would be nothing without the show.

The usual fear didn't strike. Funny, that. "Not a problem, Troy. Consider this my last show. I'm actually looking forward to seeing my ma. It's been a long time." And if she sent him away again, he would deal with it differently this time. He wouldn't yell and punch the wall in frustration. No, this time he would show her the new man he'd become. He would share the love of

God that was in him until she finally believed it for herself. Whatever it took, he wouldn't give up this time.

Colm felt the first smile he'd had on his face in two weeks.

"There! That's the look I pay you for. That's what I want to see on film. What my viewers tune in for. I'm glad to see it's still there. Now let's get moving before daylight disappears."

"Nay. I didn't finish this house for the show or for you," Colm said as he headed to the kitchen toward the side porch where Gretchen was. He wanted to share his plans with her. As much as she'd pushed him away since they kissed, he couldn't imagine sharing it with anyone else. A vision of her beside him, lending him some of her inner strength when he went to his mother again, flashed in his mind. He pushed it aside as nothing but a fanciful whimsy. Gretchen had her own new life to live now.

One on her own.

Colm walked briskly through the updated kitchen with its shiny new stainless-steel appliances waiting for Gretchen's culinary expertise. He pushed open the screened door and stepped out onto the side porch and paused. The view of the ocean far and wide brought an immediate sense of peace. It washed over him as the sunset's fiery sky took his breath away. Strokes of purples and reds brushed across the horizon.

Lord, I am so humbled by the gifts You give me and the plans You have for me. May I always stand in awe of them. Your hand in my life is just as artful and intentional as this sky in front of me.

Colm closed his eyes for a moment and saw another of God's works of art. Hair like spun gold, eyes blue like that far and wide ocean. And as distant from him as Ireland herself.

Lord, take care of her. Do whatever it takes to show her she's not meant to face life alone.

Colm thought of earlier in the week when he'd found Gretchen in the dining room attempting to hang a curtain. Her five feet wouldn't allow her to reach a foot from the window top. He'd hurried in and brought the curtain to its place with ease. It was a simple maneuver meant to help her, but when she'd turned to face him, he'd seen her no-vacancy sign in place.

Her desire to be a steadfast island would eventually isolate her beyond reach, leaving her vacant permanently. But if he would never give up on his ma, how could he give up on Gretchen?

He couldn't and wouldn't. End of story.

Colm trekked across the porch and stepped down to the grass. He'd expected to see her out here painting, but the rear yard was empty. He walked a little farther toward the barn. Voices from inside stopped him. The doors were shut, but a side window stood open. Colm recognized Ethan saying, "We're almost done, Gretchen."

Colm smiled at finding her and headed for the doors.

"This could be our last night," Ethan said. "I can't leave here with so much unresolved."

Colm halted with his hand on the latch. He didn't like earwigging, but confusion at the direction of this conversation halted him.

"What are you saying?" Gretchen's voice spilled from the window. She sounded upset as she asked the same question Colm wondered.

"I need you," Ethan responded.

Colm heard silence, but Ethan's words blared in his head.

He retracted his hand from the handle but halted when he saw his clenched fist.

Just when I thought my old self was gone.

Colm stepped back, defeated. A twig beneath his foot snapped like a firecracker. He didn't wait to see if they heard but legged it for his trailer.

"What do you need from me?" Gretchen asked after she peered out the window. She'd heard something snap and thought someone was approaching the barn, but the yard was clear all the way to the house.

"You know I've narrowed my search to the five crew members who were all on location for the other four thefts. Troy, Sly, Nate, Wendy… and Colm."

Gretchen closed her eyes and pressed her lips. She felt her shoulders sag like deflated sails. "You haven't cleared Colm? I really hoped you'd find something to turn you in a different direction."

Ethan shook his head. "He's still my number one suspect. I'm sorry, but his past is—"

"His past," she cut in. "If we are defined by our pasts, then few of us have hope for anything better. Our pasts become our chains and are worse than any jailer or bully or puppet master we could ever have to face, because escape is never possible."

Ethan sighed but said, "I have a job to do, Gretchen—bring the thief in. That's it. It's not up to me to play counselor. Not even to judge."

"How about being a friend?" she asked.

Ethan scoffed, "In my line of business, there are no friends."

She tilted her head and stared at the FBI man. He just wanted to get the arrest any way he could. "You know, you and Colm are not so different. You both live life playing someone you're not."

"Now see, I would've said you and I are more alike. We both understand we're stronger on our own."

Gretchen stood silenced. A few heartbeats pumped loudly in her head. "Right," she whispered. She'd said those words a hundred times to anyone who would listen, and even to those who wouldn't. But she had to wonder when "on her own" began to feel more like being totally alone.

The answer was obvious: when Colm came to shore.

The past two weeks had been torture. She'd done everything she could to avoid being in his presence. Their kiss had been beautiful and freeing, but she couldn't hope it would stay that way.

Especially if he was the thief fencing art. Even if he did it for his mother, to stay with him meant Gretchen would be dancing for another puppet master, and that could never happen again.

"Fine," she said, resolved. "What do you need me to do?"

"Write five notes, each one the same. They'll say, 'Meet me tonight at the rock. I want to give you what you want.' Then you'll drop them in their tool buckets and wait to see who bites."

"What if no one does?"

Ethan chuckled. "The thief is desperate. He or she will have a hard time waiting until tonight."

"So, I just go and meet whoever shows up?"

"Don't worry, I'll be in the trees, listening. You'll wear a wire. If anything happens, I'll step out and put an end to it." Ethan moved up in front of her. "It's almost over, Gretchen. Soon you'll have your big house and new business. You'll be calling the shots. You'll be in control with no one to tell you what to do ever again."

She nodded absently as he reached for her hand and rubbed his thumb over the back of her palm.

"See? I told you. You're just like me." Ethan smiled reassuringly. "On our own to the very end."

FOURTEEN

"Hanging in there?" Ethan's voice projected from the minuscule earplug. Spy equipment, Gretchen thought from her spot by the rock with the ocean at her back. Just a few weeks ago, she'd half joked about the show installing tiny cameras to catch her in accidents to spike their ratings.

If only this had been about ratings.

"Let's just get this over with," she whispered down to the tiny microphone attached under the top buttons of her pink polo shirt. "It's after ten. When do you think someone—"

A branch to her left snapped and cut off her words.

"You're on, Gretchen," Ethan whispered. "Remember, if you need me, use the code word."

Code word. She pulled it from her mind and nearly said it aloud before the scene unfolded around her. A shadow appeared at the tree line, and the word nearly spilled from her lips again.

Cut.

Fast. Simple. Powerful.

Cut.

Stop. Finished. The end.

Except this scene was just beginning.

"It's about time you came to your senses and decided to give me what I want," a low male voice said from the trees. The man had yet to step out to where she hoped the moon would give her the benefit of its natural light.

Except, whoever stood beyond the moon's reach knew how to stay in the shadows.

"I thought I was going to have to delay our departure tomorrow. You should know I don't like making delays…for anyone. I don't care how pretty she is."

Gretchen cringed at the compliment that felt more like sandpaper across a wound. The good thing about the scene was that Wendy was now off the list. But who was it?

The figure was tall like Colm, but the voice didn't match up. But then Colm was a chameleon when it came to becoming someone else. If this was he, she would have failed miserably at thinking she'd finally figured him out. Not a carpenter, but a thief.

Gretchen cleared her throat so she could answer slowly and carefully, "Sorry to keep you waiting, but I wanted my house done. I'm sure you can understand. It was business, and business comes before—"

"Pleasure," he said, cutting her off and stepping into the light. The moon illuminated Troy's face. "And now it's time for pleasure."

Gretchen shrank back on reflex, but with the ledge behind her and the crashing waves below, moving farther away wasn't an option. The pure evil she felt coming from Troy was just as perilous. She looked to the trees at her left, but she didn't have even a second to move because Troy rushed at her at full speed.

"Oh, no, you don't. You're not going anywhere until I get what I came for."

He reached for her arms and Gretchen yelled, "No, Troy!"

He pulled her to him. "Oh, yes. You've kept me waiting long enough. I've had to watch you lead McCrae around like a puppy on a leash for weeks. I want a little of that action, and I'm here to collect."

Troy smashed hard lips down on hers and drew the breath from her lungs. With his hands pushing her upper arms into her rib cage, she couldn't expand her chest even a bit.

Gretchen struggled in his grasp and whimpered as loud as she could, hoping Ethan would hear and come running as he'd promised.

But Troy's assault continued into a minute

and more. He backed her up against the rock, and she used all her strength to stay on her feet. Fear struck her lightning-quick. Never did she think she would be in this kind of danger. Where was Ethan?

Gretchen twisted her head back and forth to unseal her lips from his, and for a brief moment air found her mouth. "Cut!" she yelled. "Cut!"

Troy froze, but his grasp on her stayed strong. The next moment his chest rumbled with sick laughter. "Sorry, my dear, but there's room for only one director in this show."

Just as his lips came to hers again, she yelled, "Painting. Don't you want the painting? Isn't that what you're here for?"

"Painting? What painting?" He hovered above her like one of his microphones during filming. She wished there was a microphone. Something was seriously wrong with the one she wore if Ethan hadn't come running yet.

"I came because your little note said you wanted to give me what I wanted. Now pay up." Troy forced his lips on hers and stole what air she had left. Then his whole body tore away. One moment he crushed her, the next she stood free, the cool air flowing into her lungs.

Gasping for breath, Gretchen watched two men fight. She saw a flying fist make contact with Troy's face, forcing the director to fall back hard to the ground. She walked unsteadily to the rock and leaned against it, panting.

"What took you so long?" she asked as her breathing steadied. She closed her eyes in relief.

"I came as soon as I could, my love."

Colm? Gretchen's eyes flew open.

But Billy's angry face bore into hers. He grabbed her upper arm and dragged her toward him as his other hand ripped the buttons off her polo shirt.

"Billy! What are you doing?"

"Taking precautions."

One swipe and he had the tiny surveillance equipment in his hand, then on the ground beneath his feet. A few stomps and the cracking sound told her all lines had been cut.

"Not one word or I'll do to you what I did to him. Follow the path to the shore."

"What are you doing?"

Billy shook her enough to lift her off the ground. "Will you ever learn who is in charge? I said be quiet." With that he followed through on his threat.

Colm swept his hand down the railing of the staircase. The home was officially complete and Nate was ready to film the final scene. "She's not upstairs," Colm told him.

"Well, I guess we're filming without her. The

crew is exhausted and ready to pack up. Let's move." Nate headed into the living room with his equipment. A roaring fire in the fireplace cast a warm glow on the room. Antique furniture with its flowery upholstery sat ready for Gretchen's guests. "I'll film from this direction with the furniture behind you. Too bad the wall over the fireplace is empty. It would make for a better backdrop."

Colm thought of the painting hidden upstairs. He could quickly retrieve it for the take and put it back after.

But then the piece had already caused Gretchen so much trouble. What if someone else saw it on the telly? It could invite more danger to her shores than she already faced.

Colm moved to stand in front of the couches. "Shouldn't we wait for Troy? You know how he gets when I play director. I'm really not up for his ire tonight."

"You? Not up for a fight? Come on. You live for a good brawl." Nate brought his camera up on his shoulder and said, "And tonight, I'm playing director. Action."

The camera's abrupt light blinded Colm, and Nate's reminder of his old self silenced him. He really would never escape his past.

Nate looked at Colm around the camera. "I

said action. Let's go, I want to pack up and go home."

"We're back for our final take of the beautiful bed-and-breakfast The Morning Glory. Come next week—"

"Irish, Colm," Nate reminded yet again. "Take Two."

Colm cleared his throat. "Welcome back. I mean, we're back—"

"Cut." Nate brought the camera down with a huff. After a deep breath, he said, "All right, take five and get yourself together. I'll be in the kitchen." He put down the camera and walked out of the room.

A half-empty bottle of water lay on top of his tools by the front door. Colm grabbed it and twisted off the cap. With the bottle to his lips, he dropped his gaze to a folded piece of paper that had been beside the bottle. He picked it up and shook it open.

Colm,
Meet me at the rock tonight. I want to give you what you want.
Gretchen

Colm read through the words twice. And then again to be sure. Was this message true blue? And even if it was, did Gretchen even know what he wanted? That forever wouldn't be long enough when it came to what he wanted with her?

And what about Ethan? Wasn't there something between them? Colm remembered what he had heard by the barn. Ethan had said he needed Gretchen, not the other way around. At least not up until the point Colm left for his trailer. Perhaps Ethan's declaration made Gretchen admit her true feelings, and she realized they were for Colm, not the painter.

Colm ran for the kitchen. "Nate, let's get this over with. I have someplace to be. Nate!"

The room stood empty. The back door was open to the side porch, but peering out the screen, Colm could see that, too, was vacant.

"Nate?" he called into the darkness, but no reply returned. Not a sound.

Water lapping the side of a boat roused Gretchen from her blacked-out state—only to deliver her into throbbing pain when she attempted to open her eyes.

A groan escaped her lips and she tried to reach for her head but found she couldn't move her hands. Her mind registered quickly: *I'm tied up and blindfolded.*

The next second, pain exploded from her hip. Someone had kicked her.

"Say one word and I'll gag you, as well." Billy's voice loomed over her. "You should know by now I'll do it."

Gretchen sealed her lips, holding in her whimper of pain and the many questions flooding her mind.

Was Billy connected to the painting? Had he always known what Len had hanging on the wall? Was that why he wouldn't let her break up with him? Had he known Len planned to leave her the painting? If so, perhaps Billy planned on selling it once they were married. Only she broke off the engagement and cut his plans to shreds.

"Billy," she whispered into the darkness.

"Shh," he hissed from the other end of the boat. "I told you to be quiet. It won't be long now."

"For what?"

"You're not too bright, Gretchen. Now I have to punish you again." His footsteps neared and she felt his presence lean over her. His hand touched the top of her head and suddenly yanked her hair back at her scalp. As soon as her mouth opened in protest, he jammed a rag in, bringing tears to her eyes when she gagged.

He laughed, and in this moment she knew his abuse had nothing to do with a painting. Billy

Baker took joy in belittling her and causing her pain. He relished using violence to control her.

"You're late," Billy whispered harshly toward someone. Heavy footsteps dropped on board, tilting the boat. "I've delivered her, now give me the film." A sound that mimicked the crunching of paper reached Gretchen's ears. "Perfect. Can't let that get into the wrong hands. I'd be ruined for sure."

Footsteps drew close to Gretchen. Hot breath hit her in the face, and she knew Billy stood mere inches from her. "So long, Gretchen. If you'll excuse me, I have a certain film to torch. You don't have your proof any longer. I'd listen to this guy, though. I think he's capable of doing a lot more than cutting a few floorboards."

Billy cut her floor? She wasn't surprised to learn this. A part of her always knew he could hurt her even before he ever did.

"Yeah, I did it. I saw that bucket sitting on the porch all by itself while that stupid host walked the property. I grabbed his jigsaw to put an end to your plans. But, as it turns out, putting an end to you is better."

She felt the back of his hand brush her cheek, and she braced herself for the searing pain again. When he removed his hand suddenly, she flinched. She couldn't help it, she expected an attack. Billy's departing laughter told her he'd noticed her response, and she realized she still danced on his strings. She also realized that as a judge of character she was a failure. Which meant, for all she knew, the person Billy had just sold her to in exchange for saving his reputation could be Colm, the street-fighting thief himself.

The boat's motor roared to life. Gretchen tried to twist her body around but found Billy had not only tied her hands behind her back, he'd tied her down. Below her the deck vibrated through her whole body, and suddenly she felt the boat take off at full speed.

She screamed through the rag, twisting with all her might. She had to get off this boat before she was taken out to sea for her deadliest "accident" yet.

FIFTEEN

"Hey, Colm," Wendy said as she stepped out of her trailer with her makeup kit, "I was just coming to the house. Is Gretchen up there?"

"No, she's not. And neither is Nate. Have you seen him?" At the shake of her head, Colm scanned the yard to the trailers. Some of the windows glowed softly, but not Nate's.

Colm's watch showed it was nearing eleven o'clock. Most of the crew was eager to get off the island tomorrow, especially after Colm had pushed them full speed ahead to finish the house in time. He knew he'd exhausted them. But it wasn't over yet.

"The final scene still needs to be filmed, and I have someplace to be," Colm said. The direction of the rock where Gretchen said to meet beckoned him. Unfortunately, the silhouettes of trees blocked any view of her through the darkness.

"Apparently, I do, too. Gretchen sent me a note. I just found it." Wendy reached into her makeup kit and withdrew a slip of paper that looked just like the one Colm had in his jeans pocket. She opened it just as Colm reached for his. Side by side, they found a nearly identical message. The only difference was the names the note had been addressed to. "What does Gretchen think we want?"

The hope in Colm's heart evaporated. "Not what I thought," he muttered and looked again in the direction of the rock.

On a sigh, he turned to Sly's trailer, but the lights were out. He knew the old man wouldn't mind if he woke him up to talk. Many nights Colm had done just that, but Sly had given so much these past two weeks to help finish the house. He'd worked long days followed by all-nighters. He deserved this rest. And Colm knew what the man would say, anyway: *There's always a better way.*

"So, what is it, Sly? What's the better way to win her?"

"Pardon?" Wendy said.

"Sorry, I'm thinking out loud." He gave a halfhearted chuckle.

"Is everything all right?" she asked warily.

"Sound as a bell. I'll stroll out to the rock to find out what Gretchen wants. No need for both of us to go. Get some rest."

"So you don't think you'll be filming tonight?

If you do you know you'll need makeup. There are lots of lurking shadows to combat when filming at night."

"I can't do much filming without a cameraman. And my days of combat are over." He could only hope. "We'll have to wrap the show up in the morning before we leave. Pleasant dreams, Wendy." With that he walked past the trailers and headed out to the rock.

With every step though the pine trees, his feet treaded on a ground of soft needles in silence. This would be the last evening he would spend on Gretchen's island. Their paths would most likely never cross again. The way his chest constricted with each step, he thought he might need a puff of her inhaler before he reached her.

Except when he finally cleared the trees, he saw no one waiting for him. "Gretchen? Are you here?" he called to the darkness just as a movement off to his left caught his eye.

A man stood bent over a person lying on the ground.

"Gretchen!" Colm barreled at the man and grabbed him at the midsection. The two went down, but when Colm scrambled over to the body in the grass, he saw it was another man, not Gretchen.

"Troy?" Colm felt for the man's pulse, then swung around to see Ethan gaining his feet.

"What did you do to Troy?" A sudden surge of worry about what he didn't see at the scene pushed him to his feet. "Where's Gretchen?"

Ethan rubbed the back of his head. "It would appear I've brought danger to her doorstep."

"Appear?" Colm closed in on the man with slow steps.

"If she's dead, it's my fault."

The color red clouded Colm's vision. He grabbed hold of Ethan's denim shirt. Without realizing he even moved, he forced the man up against a tree at lightning speed. "Where…is… she?" he asked through gritted teeth.

"I don't know. She was taken. I was knocked out before I could get to her. I thought it was Troy she was fighting off, but he's been knocked out, too. Whoever hit us must have her."

"Give me one good reason why I shouldn't deck you." Colm leaned in, but before he could make a move he found the tables turned in a flash. One second he had Ethan in his grasp—the next, Colm found himself on his knees with his arms behind his back.

Fast breaths escaped his lungs. "Wh…where did you learn that takedown?" he asked incredulously. "Are you a ghetto boy, too?"

"No. FBI." Ethan reached into his pocket and withdrew a wallet. He showed the badge to Colm and let him take it all in. Ethan said,

"I'm investigating your crew for works of art that have gone missing from some of your renovations. It's no secret that someone is after a certain piece on this island, as well."

"You think someone from my crew is involved?"

"Possibly you."

"Are you mad? If I wanted the painting I would be long gone with it by now. I know where it is."

"I suppose that's true." Ethan hummed his indecision. "All right. Because I need your help finding Gretchen, I'm going to let you go. Plus, something tells me you care more about her than you do any painting. Am I right?"

Colm didn't hesitate and nodded once. "More than anything."

With that, Ethan released him and walked to a place in front of the rock. He knelt and grabbed something from the ground. "She sent notes to my five suspects. You, Sly, Wendy, Nate and Troy. Then I had her wear a wire. A lot of good it did."

Colm reached for the smashed equipment. "This is what you needed her for—bait?" He felt the roiling emotion that used to lead to an all-out brawl. The man definitely had it coming. Instead Colm turned away and said, "Time is ticking. We need to wake up everyone, crew and town. Whether Gretchen wants our help or not, she's going to get it."

They ran through the woods and started banging on the sides of trailers. Colm ran straight for Sly's mobile and barged in. "Sly! We need you. Gretchen's missing." He reached the man's bed, but when he felt around, he found it empty and still made.

Sly wasn't here.

Colm backed away from the bed, sickness flooding his body and raising bile in his throat. Was Sly involved in this?

For his friend to orchestrate Gretchen's kidnapping would mean everything the man told Colm about being forgiven would mean nothing. Colm's new life would be a lie. He really would be a phony.

"Nay. I am not a phony," Colm stated aloud and refused to let the doubtful thoughts take root. Sly was a friend, but he wasn't the one who gave Colm his forgiveness and new life. Jesus was the friend who laid down His life and saved Colm. And His promises weren't phony.

But if Sly thought stealing artwork from clients was his better way to getting rich, he had some things to pay for.

"And if he took Gretchen, he will answer to me," Colm vowed to the empty trailer.

"Colm, you in there?" a voice boomed from

outside the trailer and the door swung wide. "There you are." Sheriff Matthews stood in the doorway. Behind him hundreds of people with flashlights filed into the yard. The sight of the whole island in one place nearly knocked Colm over and struck him silent.

"We heard Gretchen's been taken," the sheriff said. "We've formed search parties, with some heading out to sea and others searching the woods."

"You've already gathered search parties? How? Ethan and I just found out ourselves."

"Your electrician came running into town, saying he saw Gretchen being carried into a boat. He'd been sitting on the shore in the shadows and was able to escape unnoticed. He came straight to me. He knew he couldn't overtake the man and it would be better to round up help."

"Of course." Air rushed from Colm's lungs with relief. "That's Sly's better way."

Colm followed Sheriff Matthews out and thanked some people for coming. Fear and worry showed on the many faces, but so did determination. They were ready for a fight, and in that moment Colm looked down at his fisted hands and noticed he was, too. He had been ready since the moment Ethan told him he'd put a wire on Gretchen.

But Colm hadn't belted Ethan as he would have in his former days.

Instead he'd set out to round up help.

The realization struck Colm as he watched the mass of people around him making plans and strategies for the coming evening just as he had in that split-second decision.

That was when it finally hit him.

His old self really was dead. He had no doubt about it now. Jesus had made him a new creation, but definitely not a weaker one. Colm still had his strength, but now he knew how a real fighter fought. It wasn't reflexive; it was responsive. It was strength and power under control, even in the chaos.

Especially in chaos.

Restoration does not take place in an atmosphere of peace, he realized. *It occurs in the midst of conflict.*

And suddenly Colm could see in the midst of the worst battle he had ever fought, fighting for the woman he loved, he had been restored. Peace flooded over him and allowed him now to fight clearheaded for Gretchen.

"Sheriff, did Sly say if he recognized the man who took Gretchen?"

"Yes, he did. I'm saddened to say it was Billy Baker. It's hard to imagine one of our own would turn on us."

"Us?"

"Yes. We feel Billy's abuse of Gretchen is an attack on us all. We trust each other, and he broke that trust."

Colm could see the island was a tight community and loved that Gretchen was a part of it. He meant to keep it that way tonight.

"I never thought he would hurt her at all," Sheriff Matthews continued as an odor wafted to Colm's nose.

He sniffed the air and turned. "Do you smell smoke?"

Colm and a few bystanders searched the area for the direction of the growing smoke scent. Quickly all noticed black billows mixing with the gray clouds of the evening.

"Fire!" someone shouted.

Colm saw smoke drifting near Gretchen's house. He legged it for the servants' quarters.

Colm passed the medical station wagon with Troy sitting on the back bumper, holding a cold pack to his face. "Stop right there, McCrae! Get Nate. I want this on film, now!" Troy tried to stand but dropped back onto the bumper.

Colm kept running. Flames burst out the back of the house, growing hotter and higher each second. The old wood of the house lit up in seconds.

His first thought screamed, *Gretchen.* Then

he remembered she was taken out to sea. To stay and fight the fire would mean not finding her.

Colm growled loudly in frustration. There was no way to save both Gretchen and her house, and right now, she came first.

But just before he turned away, he thought he saw a person running from the house into the woods. And that someone sure looked like Billy Baker.

But if it was Billy, what had he done with Gretchen?

Colm's stomach bottomed out as he took in the growing fire again.

There was no doubt now.

Sheriff Matthews ran up behind Colm and halted at the sight. "This is no coincidence."

"No, and I think I just saw Billy running from the house. There's a chance she's in there."

"As soon as the fire crew is ready, they'll check it out. We have two people to find. Troy says his cameraman is missing, as well. He might be in there, too."

"Nate's gone?"

A quick realization crossed Colm's mind. Gretchen had sent Nate a note, too.

Colm looked at the attic and the location of the painting. "Is that what you want, Nate?" Colm looked to the lawman. "Sheriff, grab your deputy. I'm going in."

If Gretchen was inside, no one and nothing would be able to stop him. Not a blazing fire or an art thief.

The rumble of the engine died out. Gretchen felt the boat glide a bit farther, but soon the choppy waves slowed it and bounced it side to side. Water hit the hull in what would normally be a soothing rhythm, but tonight as she lay bound and gagged, the sound only reminded her that she was in over her head. If she went overboard tied up, she'd never resurface. Those very same lapping waves would push her under, her hands useless.

Footsteps sounded beyond where her head lay on the deck. Her whole body tensed for whatever was to come.

Suddenly the rag in her mouth was pulled out and Gretchen screamed. She twisted in her ropes but soon figured if she was allowed to scream, it would do no good. Wherever she'd been taken, no one could hear her.

She asked, "Who are you?"

"I think the correct question is, what do I want?"

The voice was male, but she couldn't place it. It sounded familiar. She needed her kidnapper to speak more or to take off her blindfold.

"All right, then, what do you want?" Gretchen

followed his lead and hoped a few more words would match a face to the voice.

"You tell me. Your note said you wanted to give it to me."

He was one of the five who got her note.

Gretchen deduced that this wasn't Wendy. And it wasn't Troy, and it most assuredly wasn't Colm.

Or was it? Perhaps Colm had changed his voice. But even when he dropped his accent, he still held a tone that was pure Colm McCrae. It was something he couldn't cut out, like dialect, because it was a part of his identity. Little words that weren't used regularly on American soil spilled from his mouth constantly. His Irish phrases made Gretchen feel as though she frolicked in a green meadow with little thatched-roof cottages on a hillside down yonder, as he would say.

Gretchen smiled, remembering such a time, then started when her kidnapper barked, "Well? I don't have all night, and neither do you."

Not Colm. That she was sure of. Colm would say he had all the time in the world. So, if not Colm, her kidnapper had to be Sly or Nate.

She'd rarely heard either man speak—except when Nate reminded her of the terms she'd signed.

"What are the terms?" she asked, formulating an idea.

"The terms?"

It was Nate. She'd recognize that word on his lips any day. "Yes, Nate."

The next second her blindfold was ripped off. "The terms are that you're going to give me what I want. Then you're going to die."

Gretchen gulped, then answered, "I'm not giving you anything. Do you really think you'll get away with kidnapping and murder?"

"If you're not around to tell." Nate reached into his breast pocket and pulled out a pocketknife, the blade snapping out as he opened it. "I was hoping I wouldn't have to explain things, but since I have to, we'll do this the hard way." He reached for the ropes behind her and sawed through them with a couple quick jerks.

Only when he yanked her to a sitting position she found her hands were still tied behind her. He'd only released her from the ropes that bound her to the boat's deck. To do what? Throw her overboard like this? She shuffled away from Nate but came up against the port-side wall.

"You see, Gretchen, there on your little island you don't have a clear picture of the dirty world Colm and I come from. Where one does whatever he has to, to come out on top. It's not enough just to survive. People have to know you're in charge."

Nate swung her around by the arm. She felt like a rag doll in his rough grasp. He yanked her arms back, causing her to cry out in pain. "Even if that means someone gets hurt. Especially someone who gets in the way."

A searing pain emanated from her right pinky finger. Gretchen turned around. "You're hurting me!" she cried out. "What are you doing?"

"Giving you a taste of our world. And making sure you know I'll do whatever I have to, to get what I want."

"By cutting off my fingers?"

"The pinky will go first."

Pain exploded further from her finger and she cried out again.

"I gave you ample time to get out of my way, but you never left. I set up hazard after hazard so you would realize you shouldn't be on the set. Not even the shock worked! How was I supposed to carry out my job with you around?"

"Your job? I never stood in the way of filming. You reminded me constantly that I signed terms that stated I couldn't."

"Not the filming!" he burst out but quickly calmed. "The painting. It was going to be my biggest fence yet. When I saw it above the fireplace at the restaurant during the interview, I knew it was something special. And now you're going to give me what I want, just like your note said."

"You won't get away with this. The FBI is onto you."

Nate laughed. "They're not onto me. They're onto Colm. You see, I watched you leave the notes for the others. You didn't see me, but I saw you. Worked to my advantage. I told your ex where he could find you and to take out the fed in the woods, as well. Yeah, I already knew about him. That's why I knew this would be my last heist. Take the painting and never look back. And Colm would be the one to pay for it."

"I don't understand. How is Colm involved? He would never break the law."

Nate laughed. "Shows what you know. When I met him he was breaking the law. It was only because Troy bribed the cop that he got off. My friend was fired that day. Colm won that round. But I couldn't have him forgetting what he was, believing that just because he cracked jokes in front of my camera he was something special."

"That's what this is about? You wanted to make sure Colm knew he didn't succeed on his own?"

"He got a free ride because Troy saw dollar signs when he watched him fight. But now I've made sure he's going where he should have gone in the first place—to jail. I made sure all roads lead to him. And it was Gil Griffin who helped me."

"His stepfather?"

"Right after Colm joined the crew, Griffin called for Colm, but I answered the phone that day. He had a connection who was looking for art. He thought since Colm was now hanging with the swanky Hollywood types, he might come across some unique works that would bring a pretty penny. He then proceeded to lay on the subliminal threats that Colm's mother could really use his help and he better deliver.

"I told the man that Colm was a Goody Two-shoes now and a real praying man. We shared a laugh over that, then we talked about how a cameraman is really the person he should talk to about this venture. After all, no one notices the cameraman, but I notice everyone and every-thing, right down to the paintings on the walls.

"I sent Gil pictures of what I found, and he told me which ones to grab. A great opportunity had finally come my way to put Colm in the jail-house and put me in the rich house."

"So, you've made it look like Colm is the one stealing the art while you send them to Griffin."

"A tortured soul Colm is over the abuse of his ma. He would do anything to help her."

"You're sick."

He pressed the knife deeper into her finger, but Gretchen held her breath to hold in a whimper. "But I'm about to be very rich. Unless I don't show up with the painting. So where is it?"

"Don't you care that an old man fled his homeland with nothing but that painting? Do you even want to know why Griffin wants it? Have you thought how you're nothing but a puppet for someone else to control? You're only playing on someone's strings. You've been hoodwinked, Nate. Tell me, how much did Griffin promise you? Ten grand? A hundred grand? A *million*?"

His knife-wielding hand lessened its grip at her last figure. She knew she had her answer. She let out a laugh, having no reason to hold back now. This could be her last night alive.

"That's it, huh? A cool million." She turned to try to look him in the face. "It's a van Gogh, Nate.

"You agreed to steal it for a million dollars, when Griffin will sell it for a hundred million. It's probably worth a lot more." She leaned in close to him. "You feel those puppet strings strangling you yet? How about using your knife to cut those instead? You may think you're winning this fight, but the truth is no bully will ever allow such a thing. I know this for a fact."

Nate was quiet for a few moments. Gretchen's

lungs began to expand as she realized she may have convinced Nate that Gil was using him.

"Take me back, Nate. Let this go and break your connection with Griffin before you end up paying for his crimes. You can do it."

A second later, Nate yanked hard again on her hand and pressed his knife back into her wound. Gretchen bit down but the pain was too strong and she moaned. Tears filled her eyes.

"'You can do it,'" he mimicked in a singsong voice. "What do I look like? Some cameraman from a children's television show?" He pulled her back. "No. This is how it's gonna go down. You're going to tell me where the painting is. I know you know. I saw the old man bring it into your house the first day we arrived. I was heading out to take pics on the ledge, and I saw him carry a brown package that could only be the painting. Things would have gone easier for him if he had only left it on the wall of the restaurant. But when I paid him a visit, he wouldn't tell me where he stashed it…so I decked him. I turned that house upside down looking for it. You must have put it somewhere else. That's all I can figure. But where?"

"What do you plan to do with it if I tell you?"

"I'll fence the art myself and take all the money. And then I'll find Colm's father and make sure he pays for swindling me. I'll make sure Colm goes down for that, too. That won't be hard. Nobody will believe he isn't guilty."

A surge of anger rolled through Gretchen. Nate was right. Colm's past would deem him guilty even if he was nowhere near Ireland.

Nate shook her. "What are you waiting for? Tell me where it is!"

Gretchen stole a glance in the direction of the shore. That was when she saw the flames.

"Fire!" she shouted. "Nate, take me back. My house is on fire. I have to save it!"

"You should be thinking about saving your life, not a heap of kindling."

Billows of smoke took her dreams up with them. She had to get back to shore. A burst of energy shot Gretchen to her feet and out of Nate's grasp. He stood in response and she bent at the waist to plow headfirst into his stomach. But her head met the heel of his hand first.

The blow came so hard and fast that Gretchen's body could only follow the spin of her head as it whipped her to the right. Without the ability to brace herself with her arms, she fell flat to the deck in a painful smack.

Her whole body ached with the impact, her lungs expelled in a whoosh. As hard as she tried, she couldn't get them to refill. Then Nate was upon her again.

His blade cut into another finger, but the pain

from her fall took precedence. "Tell me where the painting is or I'll cut it off!" he shouted. "Every thirty seconds you'll lose another one."

Gretchen tried to look toward the shore. Her life was going up in flames. Her dreams of independence were over…unless she told him the painting was in the house.

As air slowly seeped back in, her reasoning became clear again. If she told Nate, he would take her back to get it before it perished in the fire. He wouldn't let *his* dream go up in smoke.

But could she let hers?

SIXTEEN

Gretchen knew what she had to do.

She closed her eyes and let her dreams burn away.

Billy had said he was going to torch the evidence of his brutality. He had just neglected to say he would torch it along with her house. She wasn't surprised at his actions. They fit well with his identity. But she was surprised that her decision to release her dreams didn't leave her feeling like a weakened victim.

The ability to turn her face filled her with power.

"Twenty-five!" Nate's voice rang through her head like a bell from a boxing ring.

Not weak, but meek. Strength under control. A winner knew there would be sacrifices. Painful ones at that. But when it was all over, she would rise from the ashes. For now, she had a fight to engage in.

"Untie me, and I'll take you to the painting.

It's treacherous out here with all the submerged rocks. I'll need to navigate carefully."

"Do I look like an idiot? I'm not untying you."

"Do you want your painting or don't you? Besides, what am I going to do, jump into the deep, black ocean? No one would ever find me. I'd never be heard from again."

"That's the plan," Nate said snidely. "But fine, I'll let you drive us in." He wrenched her to her feet and cut the ropes, then threw her toward the helm. "One wrong move and I'll cut you."

"Wouldn't think about it," she replied with her head held high. She ignored the painful sores and sticky blood on her wrists and fingers. "Besides, that's your MO, right?" Gretchen took the wheel and moved the throttle to put the boat in motion. "Stage a few mishaps for the camera, keep the light off you? You really had me going, though, when you filmed Billy hitting me. I never dreamed it was for profit. You staged that to let me think you were on my side. I think I'm starting to see what you mean about coming out on top. You'll use whatever means you can to get there."

Gretchen saw the lit lighthouse dead ahead, got her bearings and brought the boat in line with it. The lighthouse's beacon warned seafarers to stay away from the dangerous rocks that surrounded the island, but tonight its light pulled her forward and drew her eyes up.

Way up.

"We'll be going to the top tonight. Of that." She pointed to the lighthouse.

"That's where you hid it?" The beacon flashed on Nate's face as it circled around. His look of delight nearly made her forfeit the fight right then and there. The light gleamed on his expression for only a few seconds, but it was enough for her to know that if she took him up there, she would most likely come down a faster, more direct route than the way they ascended.

Especially when he realized the painting wasn't there.

Gretchen dared not turn to see her house. She might lose her focus and cave in at the sight. She needed to hold off revealing her final play until she knew for sure he could never get his hands on the painting. And she would know this only when she had lost it all.

Gretchen slowed the boat and let it drift to the large rock the lighthouse stood on about five hundred yards from land. The boat banged against the stone, and she dropped anchor. The next second, Nate had her by the strap of her painter's overalls. He pulled with a roughness that had her scraping her hands along the barnacles stuck to the rocks as she tried to keep on her feet.

Nate led her to the door, but it was locked. "How do you get in?"

She knew, having lived here her whole life, that a key was hidden. As a teenager she'd learned the not-so-secret hiding place on a late-night excursion.

"It's in the lantern hanging beside the door."

The door scraped open on rusty hinges, and the beacon from above shed some light down the spiral staircase on them.

"Ladies first." Nate gave her a shove onto the first step.

Gretchen righted herself. "Who said chivalry was dead?"

"Funny, you don't come across as a woman who wants a man to hold the door for her. I was just obliging your claim to independence. Now get moving."

As she took the first step alone, her independence felt more like isolation out here on this rock far from the townspeople's help. From Colm. "Right about now I would take that knight in shining armor," she mumbled.

"Then you shouldn't have picked a street urchin. They don't get to be knights. Keep walking."

Nate's slander cut her as deeply as if he'd attacked her personally, as if…?

As if she and Colm were one?

But that wasn't possible. How could she be independent *and* with someone?

As Gretchen led the way up the narrow metal stairs, each step she took brought a sharp ache to her heart at the idea of never seeing her Irishman again.

Her Irishman. Listen to her. She chastised herself for taking such liberties, even in thought.

And yet she knew she always would think of him as hers. Colm had given her so much of himself. He'd infiltrated her life even when she promised never to allow it again.

How had he done it?

With his smiles and selflessness.

Gretchen reached the top landing and entered a circular room enclosed in glass. Outside the glass was a narrow walkway with a short railing. She knew that all Nate had to do was scoop her up and give her a toss.

But not before she dealt the final blow.

One look out the window and she could see the flames shooting up into the sky from behind the pine trees. Her house was engulfed and it was time to hit Nate right where it would hurt him the most.

"There's nothing up here but a bunch of tools," Nate growled. "Is this some sort of trick? Did you think I wouldn't throw you over?"

Gretchen kept her gaze locked on where her house was situated on the cliff behind the trees. "No trick," she said. "Just taking your advice to make sure no one else comes out on top." She turned to look straight at him.

"Including you. You see, we both lose tonight. I've lost my house and my future. And you, well, you've lost the painting. It's in my attic. Or I should say, was." She nodded to the flames.

Gretchen half expected him to retaliate as Billy would: a right-handed slap across her face. She kept her head held high.

"It can't be. I tore that place apart, right down to the studs. You're lying."

"Lying would be cheating, and that wouldn't be fair, would it? No, Nate. If I have to lose tonight, so do you."

"Not if I can help it. Move it."

Gretchen started at his grasp and violent pull toward the stairs. "Where?"

"To the house. You're going in to get it. And if you're too late, you'll burn with it."

Colm coughed as he crawled along the floor of the servants' quarters. He had called out to Gretchen so many times he was hoarse. Flames roared around him as he made his way through, dodging shoots of fire and mounting heat. His eyebrows had to be scorched off by now. Thankfully, one of the islanders thought to drape a wet blanket over him before he ran inside. It shielded him while he searched for Gretchen…and Nate.

In a crawl through the first floor, darting around bursts of flame from the basement, Colm realized they weren't in here. If he could he would have breathed a sigh of relief, but he needed to look everywhere first. Would the fire have spread to the main house? Or had the islanders been able to contain it?

Smoke billowed around him so thickly he could only feel his way through the apartment. Colm knew the layout like the back of his hand, having pored over the blueprints for nearly a month. He reached the back staircase that would take him to the second-floor bedroom and to the main part of the house.

The entrance to the stairwell was open at the bottom, but the top was closed off by a door. Once the fire reached that doorway, there would be no stopping the beast.

The Morning Glory would never open for business.

Colm hesitated before opening the door. Even with the blanket, he felt as if he were burning inside and out. Sweat poured off him, giving the smoke something to stick to. He was sure he looked as blackened as the house. The sight would kill her, he knew: her whole future charred away.

But she wouldn't have a future at all if he didn't find her soon.

"Gretchen!" He listened intently for any human sound.

Colm pulled himself up the stairs as he watched the flames nip at his feet. He covered his eyes where the blazing orange heat scalded him and raced to get away from it. At the top of the stairs, he burst through the door and fell flat on his face. He kicked immediately to slam the door behind him, but not before flames shot out and ignited the throw rug in a loud whoosh. Colm jumped to his feet and backed away just as the flames sped toward him and the new curtains beside him disintegrated in a flash.

Colm looked at the door across the room. As soon as he opened it, the fire would retreat through it. But going back the way he came wasn't an option. He ran forward, through the door before the fire found the next flammable item.

Him.

Colm slammed the door behind him. He removed the wet blanket and draped it at the base of the door. Hopefully, the saturated towel would hold back the smoke and flames for a little longer.

The air around him cleared, and he took the reprieve from ingesting toxic smoke, still wondering how the islanders were faring. Had they put any of the fire out?

"Goldie, finding you alive is my only concern." He raced around the balcony, not touching the restored railing. It, too, would be gone soon, overtaken by the blaze that destroyed everything in its path.

Colm pushed open every door to find beautifully decorated rooms, but no people. He rushed to the attic door and pulled it wide.

Darkness loomed and he nearly wept when he reached the rooms and found them empty. If not here, then where was she?

Nate would have wanted the painting, Colm reasoned, and he raced for the trap door. If the painting was still there, then they hadn't come here. Thankfully, he still wore his barely used hammer. Tonight it would be used well. He lifted the door and dropped to his knees.

"It's still here." Dread filled Colm as he looked out through the window above him as though it would show him where they were. Had Gretchen led Nate to an unknown place to trick him?

If that was the case, Colm might never find her in time.

* * *

"Get down," Nate growled when they came in view of her burning house. He pushed Gretchen's shoulder down hard, and she fell to her elbows and knees.

The sight before her kept her there.

Hundreds of people were wrestling with the flames, make that hundreds of *islanders*. They were working together to put out the fire!

But why?

She watched people spraying hoses from the fire trucks' tanks. Many passed buckets in an assembled line, then passed them back to be refilled.

She wished she could call out from where Nate had her hidden in the darkness, but no one would hear her over the roar of the fire or their shouts. Maybe if she broke out of the clearing and away from Nate, she could find refuge in the masses, but before she could plan her next step, Nate dragged her back into the woods.

"Where are we going?" she asked.

"Around to the front. I said you were going to burn. I didn't say I was."

She noticed the flames were contained to the rear of the house. "All because of the islanders," she said aloud, her mind still reeling at the thought of them helping her when they had been against the B&B from the beginning.

Nate gave her a shove. "Move. I want that painting before it goes up in flames."

Gretchen stayed behind the tree line but took in the scene with question after question. Questions that she would never know the answers to because as she skirted her property, she knew she walked to her death. Once Nate had the painting, it would be all over for her unless she came up with another tactic to free herself.

They reached the front of the property. "It's all clear," Nate growled. "We're going right through the front door, and I don't want a word out of you. Got it?"

Gretchen nodded, but just in case, Nate covered her mouth with his foul, beefy hand. All she could hope was that someone would see them.

Her hope was in vain.

They walked right up the steps and through the door without notice. As soon as they were inside, Nate flashed his knife to point the way up and shoved her forward.

"I'm not dying in this fire tonight, so you better make it quick," he instructed. "This part of the house is already filling up with smoke."

At the second floor Gretchen noticed where the smoke poured from under the door that led to the servants' quarters. The fire had to be right behind it.

A cry escaped her lips, but she bit it back and turned her gaze from the sight. There was no use saving the house if she didn't save herself. And she had to keep Len's painting out of Nate's hands. She couldn't let him run off with it tonight, never to be heard from again.

Gretchen had to wonder if Len would rather the artwork burned in the fire than got stolen by crooked dealers. After all he went through to save it from the hands of tyrants, would it be better to eliminate its existence forever?

Gretchen passed by her bedroom and through the smoke noticed the door was open. In fact, all the doors were, she saw as she scanned the upstairs balcony. That was when she noticed the railing was completed. Colm had restored it along with her home, bringing the structure back from abandonment. For so long the house had lain lonely and vacant with no hope of anything more in its future. The longer people ignored it, the more disgrace befell it. Until she recognized how it felt, being so much like it.

Then Colm came along and restored it with his talented hands. What a gentle, loving touch could do! The house blossomed around her and a sense of freedom shone from floor to ceiling. Its state of permanent vacancy was lifted. All because of Colm. But not because he wanted anything from it. He gave freely with no strings attached.

Gretchen realized then that something could be free only when it was in the care of someone who demanded nothing from it. And she had her answer about the painting.

Rescue it.

She also suddenly wanted the same for her life. Colm had proven that real love did exist and she could have it without strings. That in fact his love rejoiced in her living freely.

But that meant Gretchen had to have a life in which to live freely. That meant she had to get out of this dangerous situation alive. She would have to do whatever was necessary to escape.

"Nate, I have to get the crowbar from my room. It's the only way to open the latch."

"Hurry up!" At first she thought he might let her go in alone. She hoped to break a window and call for help.

But Gretchen turned and saw him right on her heels. She stretched her mind to think of another tactic. No time to dwell on the losses.

And that was when she had an idea and let out a choking cough.

The smoke was pouring around her more rapidly now, and in a few minutes the cough wouldn't have to be faked. But if she could convince Nate now that she was incapable of going farther, she might escape.

Gretchen reached for the crowbar by the

door. She wheezed and clutched her chest. "My asthma… I'm getting…an attack… Smoke… too much."

He ripped the crowbar from her with one hand and grabbed her upper arm with the other. "Nice try."

"Really. Can't breathe."

"Doesn't matter. You only have to live until I have the painting. So be quick about it, so I can get out and you can get to dying."

"No!" She struggled to free her arm as he pulled her through the hall and to the attic door. "Please! I want to live."

"Suddenly your asthma's gone. How convenient! Get upstairs *now*."

She led the way, realizing her slip. She wouldn't be able to escape from the attic again. And now she would have to give him the painting, too.

"Where is it?" he demanded when they entered the room at the top of the stairs.

Gretchen hesitated but soon felt the crowbar pushing into the side of her head. On a whimper, she led Nate to the spot. "It's in the floor. There's a hiding place, but I have to bend down to feel for it."

"Then do it."

She knelt and with trembling fingers she found the raised board. "Right here. Use the crowbar to lift this piece." *Then my life will end*, she thought.

The hinges creaked and she heard Nate rummage around in the dark. "Where is it?" he shouted. "I don't feel anything."

Gretchen leaned forward to feel inside the compartment. "I don't understand. It was right inside here."

Pain exploded from her scalp. Nate had a fistful of her curls. "I told you I didn't want any more of your games. Now, where's the painting?" he shouted.

"Someone else must have stolen it."

"Then I guess I have no reason to keep you alive."

Gretchen held her breath and waited for the crowbar to find its mark. She let out a whimper of a prayer, but before she finished saying *Please, God, help me*, she heard a click and a lightbulb burned bright.

The first thing she saw was Nate with the crowbar held high over her head.

Then she heard an Irish voice that sounded better than music to her ears: "Looking for this, love?" Colm stood with the painting in his hands.

Gretchen let out a wail and tried to crawl around Nate to get to Colm, but Nate wasn't having it. Gretchen ducked her head and covered herself with her hands, expecting Nate to hit her.

"Don't do it, Nate," Colm said quietly, but she didn't miss the lethal tone in his voice. "Take the painting and go."

"And leave you two alive to tell? I don't think so! The both of you will disappear tonight and all will think you stole it together." Nate lifted the crowbar higher.

Gretchen grabbed her chest and gave a painfully loud wheezing sound. She fell at Nate's feet.

Nate kicked her as she gripped her chest, giving short, loud breaths.

"Look, Colm, your weak little girlfriend is having her final asthma attack. I'm surprised you like her so much. She would never have survived on the streets. And she would've definitely kept you down. But knowing how much you do like her, I'm tempted to let you watch her writhe on the floor until she takes her last breath."

Gretchen's whole body convulsed and shook against the wood floor.

"Let me help her, Nate!" Colm yelled, his voice rumbling through the rafters.

Gretchen peeked up to see Nate holding Colm back. But she also saw the way Colm's muscles were tensed. He could easily take Nate down, but if he did that, he might kill the man. Colm was that angry. For weeks he said he would never fight again, but in this moment, she knew if he did, it would be to the death.

Gretchen couldn't let him make such a sacrifice, especially when she was faking the asthma attack. But their lives were still in danger.

Before Colm could make his move, Gretchen lifted her legs and jammed them into Nate's gut. The man lost his balance and his hold on Colm. Gretchen jumped to her feet just as Colm threw the painting to her.

"Take it and go!" he shouted and shot out an arm to grab the crowbar from Nate.

Nate held fast. The two men locked hands on the tool, faces inches apart. Two street fighters with the smarts to fight dirty...and lethally.

"Go, Gretchen!" Colm said through gritted teeth, holding Nate back with all his might.

"And let you kill him?" she shouted. "No! You'd never forgive yourself!"

"Not if I kill him first," Nate answered and crashed his forehead against Colm's.

Colm yelled out in pain, and Gretchen thought he might fall back and lose his hold. But his arms stayed strong and the next second he pried at Nate's wrist and got a hold strong enough to twist it in an unnatural way. Nate screamed as his arm followed his hand to near breaking. Then Nate rammed the crowbar into Colm's kneecap, and a loud crack echoed through the attic.

Colm went down on his good knee with a grunt.

"Colm!" Gretchen yelled. She wanted to go to him but getting in the mix would only complicate matters. No, there was only one way to help him. "Fight, Colm! Fight him! He'll kill us!"

Colm didn't take his eyes off Nate, especially with the burly man standing over him with the crowbar still in his hand. Gretchen couldn't miss the change in Colm's expression at her words. Her permission set him free.

Colm went for one of Nate's legs, yanking one forward at the same moment his other hand jammed the man's rib cage. The crowbar flew out from the man's hands as he grabbed his broken ribs and fell to his knees.

But Nate wasn't out yet. With both men now on their knees, he reached for Colm's throat and Gretchen stepped forward to stop him. Before she could interfere, Colm blocked the assault with an elbow to Nate's arm and another hand to Nate's nose. The impact sent his head back in a snap. He quickly brought it back, ignoring the blood spurting from his face, but Colm dealt another blow, fast and furious.

Colm was prepared to kill tonight, and he would.

Unless she interfered.

She noticed that Colm leaned in to his attacker

to give himself more leverage and to weaken
Nate's blows, but that didn't give her a clear
opening to any part of Nate's body.

Then she remembered the crowbar had fallen.
She moved around the wrestling men to search
the floor for the tool. She couldn't find it. It must
be in a dark corner, she figured, and she didn't
dare turn her back on the men.

Gretchen looked down at the painting in her
hands, then looked up and saw Nate held Colm
back by the neck. Colm's throat gurgled. Nate
was choking the life out of him.

Without a second thought Gretchen lifted the
painting and brought it down on Nate's head.
The corner of the canvas bent on impact.

Nate stilled for a second, and his choking
hold on Colm's neck loosened. Then he lost
consciousness and fell to his side, right into the
open trapdoor.

All was quiet in the attic as shock set in. Then
as Gretchen took a step toward Colm, he, too,
crumbled to the floor.

SEVENTEEN

It was the worst dream he'd ever had. He was filming on some location, but there wasn't a house, just a lot of fog swirling around him. Troy was there, taunting him about losing the fight.

What fight? Colm pondered as he heard a distant and familiar voice. "Goldie, is that you?" He turned around and saw nothing through the fog. "Where am I? Gretchen!"

He felt a strong pull on his arm, but no one was beside him. The world started to fade to black, but Gretchen called and pulled him back to the scene. As absurd as this dream was, he had no intention of waking from it. Not with Goldie in it. She was talking to him again, and he didn't want to do anything to ruin it. One wrong move and she might turn away. One misconstrued attempt at being helpful, and she might think he was usurping her independence again.

Not that he ever meant to do any such thing.

They would make a great team, he just knew it. She was strong on her own, but they could be so much stronger together. If only she would see this. If only she would listen. And if only she would stop yelling.

Her rising voice showed a mounting hysteria. Something was wrong. This shouting was so out of character. Colm twisted around to find her, but the movement sent an excruciating pain radiating from his left knee. The agony invaded the dream and tore him away from Gretchen.

"No! Stay with me, Gretchen!"

Panic welled up as he attempted to hold on to her with all his might. Colm searched through the fog until it choked him and cut off his strength even more than the aggrieved knee. His lungs burned, but the pain only magnified knowing Gretchen lived with this looming threat of stolen air daily, when so much of her life had already been taken from her. He wouldn't call her a victim—Gretchen would go a row with him if he ever insinuated such a thing. No, she was a fighter, just as he was. But that also meant he would fight to the death for her.

Suddenly a camera appeared in front of him and Nate's face leered from behind it. And just as quickly, Colm remembered he had been doing just that—fighting to the death for her.

On a long wheezing inhale, Colm coughed his

way back to reality. As he opened his eyes, the fog from his dream clouded his vision.

Not fog, but smoke.

"Gretchen!" He felt the pull on his arm that he had felt in his dream, only now he saw her hand. She was pulling him with all her might.

"Help me! Somebody help me!" she shouted.

"Gretchen!" He called to her again, now more pronounced. He tugged back on her arm to get her attention, and the next second, her face broke through the smoke.

Colm reached for her stricken face and hoped she wouldn't turn away from him again. His palm rested against her cheek.

"Oh, Colm, thank God you're awake! I need to get you out of here. The fire is getting closer."

Fire. Colm jerked to alertness and pushed up on his arms. The pain from his dream shot to his knee again. He reached for where the throbbing tormented him. "My knee," he said.

"It's broken." She touched his neck where another sting emanated. "But I thought he had choked you to death. I thought you were…" She dropped her forehead to his and he noticed the shortness of her breath and the way air barely filled her lungs.

"I have to get you out of here." Colm clenched his teeth and ignored his pain. He hated to use her last strength to assist him.

On his feet, she put his arm around her shoulder and led him to the top of the stairs. A look below at the closed door with smoke seeping from the gap on the bottom caused Colm to pause. "Goldie, I'm going to assume the fire is behind that door. I want you to promise me you—"

"No, stop it. Just focus on getting downstairs. We'll figure the next step when we get there."

"There won't be any time." He forced her to look at him. "You're to leave me. You understand? Get out of the house and save yourself. You need to do as I say."

"You know I have a hard time doing that." Her smile trembled into a frown, but Colm chuckled at her attempt to make light of her strong will. "After tonight, you can go back to being in charge."

At her nod, he hobbled down each tread, the smoking door looming closer and closer. When they finally reached it, Colm felt the door and was surprised it wasn't hot. The doorknob was the same.

"Stand back," he instructed, but before he could turn the knob, the door flung wide and Ethan nearly plowed him over.

"Colm! Gretchen!" When Ethan noticed that Gretchen was holding him up, he reached for Colm. "I had hoped you were up here. I didn't want to believe— Come on. The fire's contained in the servants' quarters, but it's dangerous out here with the smoke."

"Still? I thought for sure by now the fire would have reached the main house," Colm said as the man led them out into the hall. The sight there told them what had held it back, or rather who.

The islanders formed a water system of various means of buckets and hoses and manpower to keep the flames from coming any farther. But as much as Colm was surprised, it didn't come close to the wonder on Gretchen's face.

Ethan ushered them down the staircase alongside the townspeople busy saving Gretchen's home and straight out the front door. A woman filling buckets to hand off saw Gretchen and ran up to her, arms stretched wide.

The sight of Gretchen enveloped by a friend allowed Colm to get back to business. He said quietly to Ethan, "Nate's in the attic. He's your man. He might need a little reviving. Gretchen knocked him out with the painting, of all things."

Ethan smiled. "I'm on it." He turned to head back into the house but stopped when Colm reached for a bucket to join the islanders. "What do you think you're doing? You should get checked out and off that leg."

"I will, after. But as long as I have breath

in me, that fire won't come any closer to the main house."

Ethan looked at Gretchen hugging another woman. "Hate to break it to you, but she's an on-her-own kind of gal."

"I wouldn't want her any other way."

"Yes, but the question is, would she want you?"

Gretchen sniffed and swiped at the tears running down her face, partly caused by the burning smoke, but more from the outpouring of love by her islanders.

"I don't understand," she said to Miriam Matthews. "Why is everyone doing this? Why are they helping me save my house when they were all so against my restoring it in the first place?"

Miriam read Gretchen's lips and lifted her hands to sign her reply. "Simple," she said. "You never asked for our help."

These words of truth seeped into Gretchen's mind. She had been so bent on claiming her independence that she left the islanders, her family, out of her plans, never thinking they might want the same thing for her. And now here they all were helping to put the fire out and save her home and business. They didn't want to keep her down—they wanted her to succeed.

More tears rolled down Gretchen's face, but

Miriam thrust a bucket into her hands and said with her loving smile, "Those won't put the flames out. Time to get busy."

Gretchen sniffed one last time with a nod, then jumped in to assist. It felt like hours before the fire chief said the flames were officially out. The roar of applause gave Gretchen shivers. They were so excited and happy for her. But with a quick glance around the mayhem of hugging and cheering, Gretchen looked for one person.

She spotted him across the front lawn, leaning against the porch railing, his injured leg impeding him from going anywhere. She began to walk to him, but as she closed in, her throat tightened against all she needed to say.

Colm's face was blackened with soot and his eyelids drooped with exhaustion, but when she stepped up in front of him, his face broke into a huge smile, his white teeth a stark contrast to his face.

"I can't believe you went back in to help put the fire out. No, wait." She held up a hand. "Actually, I can believe it. You've been nothing but helpful to me since day one. I'm sorry I didn't recognize this most honorable trait in you. I was so focused on establishing my identity I neglected to honor you for yours. Can you forgive me?"

Colm's eyebrows hitched up. "Nothing to forgive," he said with a shake of his head. "But you know, Goldie, you could have just asked me who you were. I would have told you."

Gretchen tilted her head a bit. Did she really want to know who he saw? What if he saw her as some wimpy girl, trying to play grown-up? "I'm afraid to ask."

Colm reached out and lifted her chin. She hadn't even realized she'd lowered it—an old habit. "I see a wise fighter," he said, and that was when she noticed he was speaking with his accent, thicker than ever. Before she could mention it, he continued, "I see your beautiful inner strength, Gretchen. Your *neart istigh*. It's your power, and I pray you always let it lead."

His finger stayed beneath her chin. She didn't dare even blink in case he pulled away. "I want what you see to be true."

"Aye. It is."

"But it hasn't been. I've confused strength with independence, pushing away all my loved ones to prove I could make it on my own. I haven't been very wise. But that's all going to change, starting right now."

Colm smiled, his eyes sparkling. "You are so loved, Gretchen."

Gretchen's heart expanded in her chest. Was Colm telling her he loved her? He'd implied it in the attic when they'd kissed. But it was his actions that spoke even louder than his kind words.

With every whack of his hammer and every curtain he hung for her, he showed his love. It was selfless and never smothering or controlling. The fact that he never asked anything from her revealed this, and Gretchen let this proof push her to a place she had vowed never to go again.

"I love…your accent." *Whoa*. This was harder than she thought.

"My accent? Oh, I didn't even realize I was using it. I'm exhausted. I'm sorry. I can't control it well when I'm weak."

A laugh erupted from Gretchen's throat. "You? Weak? Never. And, Colm, your accent is part of who you are. Don't change it for anybody. Be proud of your heritage. You're a handsome, rough and tough Irishman who loves to help others."

"You're blessed to have a whole island of people who want to help you. Look around you, Goldie. I meant what I said. You're loved. Every single one of these people wants to help you. Let them."

Gretchen felt disappointment sink through her. He hadn't been speaking about his feelings for her after all. He'd meant only the islanders' love for her.

Gretchen kept her chin up. She knew she still had to tell him how she felt. Even if he didn't love her back, she would always know she'd told him.

"So, I guess this is farewell," he said. "I'll be going on in the morning. Don't worry about Billy. Sly told me Sheriff Matthews has him in custody. He'll never bother you again. You're free, Gretchen. Free to live your life to the fullest, making your own decisions and calling all the shots."

Colm leaned in and placed a gentle kiss on her cheek. He lingered there and she felt his eyelashes flutter on her skin. She took a deep breath and said into his ear so close to her lips, "I love you, Colm McCrae. I love you."

At first Colm stilled. He didn't pull away, but he didn't say anything. Gretchen waited for any sign of a response, their cheeks flush against each other's.

Slowly Colm pulled away, but he wasn't looking at her. Instead, he looked beyond her, then above her. He twisted to steal a glance behind him. He came back around with wide eyes stark white in his black face and asked, "Am I on camera?"

Gretchen laughed aloud and shook her head. "No, it's just the two of us. And my islanders, of course."

"Just the two of us. And your islanders. I really like the sound of that. Marry an island woman, and you marry the whole island, as they say in Ireland."

"Is that what you want? To marry me?"

"Yes," he whispered. "I want you forever. I love you, Gretchen Bauer, and I want to grow old with you right here on Stepping Stones Island at The Morning Glory B&B. I want to sit on the back porch and watch every sunset, cuddled up with you in my arms."

He paused and grew serious. "I want you, but I don't want you ever to feel like you don't have choices in your life."

"I do have a choice. I choose you."

Colm exhaled and filled his arms with her. He whispered in her ear, "I must be dreaming."

"Then I am, too, and I don't want to wake up."

"Then it's a good thing we'll own a bed-and-breakfast, aye?"

"Aye." She smiled. "A very good thing."

"You won't be sorry, Goldie."

"How could I be? You've brought me peace, Colm. That's all I ever wanted. Oh, and I also want a fall wedding right here at The Morning Glory. I want to walk down that beautiful staircase you poured your heart into and made for me with your strong hands. I want—"

"All right, all right." Colm pulled Gretchen

close into his chest, his arms wrapping around her in a great big hug. "I see you have everything all planned out. Silly me for thinking you might need my help."

Gretchen lifted up on her tiptoes. Their lips were close, but it wasn't a kiss she was looking for. She met him eye to eye and with a look so determined he would never doubt her again, she said, "I'm no fool. I will always take your help."

Colm smiled and leaned in, their lips inches apart. Apparently, he *was* looking for a kiss. He stopped just before they touched and said, "I always knew you were a smart woman. *Tabhair póg dom.*"

She raised her eyebrows. "More of your sweet talking?"

"Aye. The sweetest in all the land, in fact."

"What does it mean?"

"It means," he said, his eyes watching her lips, "give me a kiss."

Gretchen smiled. "I'll have to remember those words," she said and gladly gave him what he wanted.

EPILOGUE

"You're sure you're not mad, Len?" Gretchen stood back as Colm hung the van Gogh over the fireplace where all the guests of The Morning Glory could see it for years to come. Even with the small dent on the corner.

"Mad? Not at all. We all have our battle scars to prove we fought the good fight, so why shouldn't the painting? It did well, and now I know for sure that I chose wisely for you to be its owner."

Tildy grunted from her place on the couch by the Christmas tree. "You all seem to forget that now I have a vacant wall over my fireplace at the restaurant. What am I supposed to put in that space?" She nudged the thin, frail woman beside her who was Colm's mother. Emily Griffin gave a small, brief smile but quickly looked down at her folded hands in her lap.

It took some doing, but Colm had eventually convinced his ma to start her life over on

Stepping Stones. Along with Nate and Billy, Gil was doing time in prison. Emily's now ex-husband was out of her life forever. Yet every time Gretchen looked at the woman, her heart broke. The trauma was still fresh in her. Every now and then, Emily would steal a glance at the sea and Gretchen knew the woman was fighting her battle. All Gretchen could do was love her mother-in-law unconditionally and let her know she understood. She would remind Emily that bonds could be broken, but there were also good bonds, ones that reflected relationships based on love and respect and support. Ones that allowed a person to live free. She would tell her mother-in-law that was what she wanted to be for her, and Gretchen vowed she would tell her this every day until the woman held her head high and believed it.

Gretchen turned and realized Colm had caught her looking at his ma. The understanding passed between them, and he offered her a sweet smile of gratitude. Gretchen sighed and walked over to her Irish husband and welcomed his arms around her. She rested her cheek on his chest for a moment before gazing up at him. She felt his strong arms tighten around her, but instead of feeling confined by those arms, she felt the assurance of his presence in her life.

Gretchen knew that somewhere deep inside

he feared she might change her mind someday and choose the solitary life. But Gretchen hoped that tonight she could put his mind at rest, just as he had brought rest to her whole life.

It had been months since her last asthma attack, and though she still carried her inhaler as a precaution, Gretchen had never breathed easier. No longer did she need to prove to the world that she was smart enough and strong enough to make it on her own, although her plumbing and electrical expertise did come in handy when they turned the attic into their own personal living quarters.

Colm had worked all summer repairing the fire and water damage. Not even a broken kneecap could stop him. He wanted The Morning Glory to have at least one season of success, and when fall came, the rooms were filled and the breakfast table bustled with impressed guests who quickly booked their spring getaways on Stepping Stones. Gretchen now had "regulars" and looked forward to hanging her no-vacancy sign.

Of course, without the attic to rent out, income was cut down. To help, Colm opened his own carpentry business and turned the barn into his workshop. Gretchen hadn't thought too much of the idea until Emily arrived and saw Colm working just as his da had. The woman cried

outright, but the smile on her lips told them the sight brought her pure joy. She no longer worried about her son, who had changed from a street fighter into a sweet man. Seeing Colm use his hands to make an honest living was the second gift Emily had received.

Gretchen couldn't wait to give the woman her third tonight.

But first to tell Colm.

As though he knew she had something to share, he led her away from the crowd of family and friends there to celebrate Christmas Eve.

Colm stopped in the foyer. "I see the wheels turning in your mind. That could only mean you're making more plans. I love a woman who knows what she wants, and you know whatever it is, all you have to do is ask. Your wish is my command."

Gretchen frowned. "I don't want to command you. Ever. We're a team with the same goal, to strive for full restoration together through encouragement and God's freeing peace inside us."

A sheen of unshed tears showed in Colm's eyes as he reached over and pulled her forehead to his. "You make me feel stronger than any brawl I've ever won. It makes me want to give you the world."

The room full of people faded into the back-

ground of twinkling lights while the Christmas music softly played.

Gretchen tilted her head. "Not the world, but how about new servants' quarters?"

He started and frowned. "You don't like the attic?"

"It's beautiful," she said quickly to put his mind at ease. "Your handiwork is as smooth as your words. I look forward to growing old with you while you sweet-talk me all day long. It's just we'll need more space."

"Oh, I see. You're concerned about not making enough money if we don't rent the attic suite. Love, I have enough restoration work to last me ten years. Everyone on the island has hired me to work on his home. After seeing ours, they all want to make Stepping Stones stand out as a real classy place for the tourists. So don't you worry your pretty golden head over it. We'll also start getting more calls once the show airs next month. It was grand that the new director and host incorporated our old footage with some of their new. He told me they're saving it for Sweeps Week. That will draw huge ratings for them and give us lots of exposure. So you see, we won't need the attic to make ends meet. The phone will be ringing off the hook."

Gretchen bit her lower lip. This was not going the way she'd planned.

Colm lifted her hand with the wedding ring on it and kissed it. The shiver he sent up her arm made her whole body tremble and she lost her train of thought. This was *really* not going the way she had planned. Life with Colm had a way of going off course.

And as always Gretchen quickly came up with plan B.

"Mom," she called over her shoulder while she smiled at Colm. "I think I have an idea of what you can hang over your fireplace."

"Well, spill it," Tildy called back. "I'm all ears."

Gretchen took a deep breath and said, "Baby pictures. The first one will be available in seven months."

The conversations stilled. Only the music still played.

A deep chuckle from over by the fireplace broke the silence. Len's laugh grew louder. "Well, well, well, what are you waiting for, son? Didn't you hear your wife? You're going to be a father."

Colm's face drained of all color as he gulped and looked from Len to Gretchen then to each face in the room. Owen and his wife, Miriam, grinned ear to ear, but it was the full smile Colm's ma wore that seemed to spark his understanding.

"This is for real? No fooling shenanigans."

Tildy hooted and hollered with excitement and jumped to her feet to run to her daughter.

Colm moved back still in a daze as the women embraced, but Gretchen tightened her hold on his hand that she could feel starting to tremble. Her mother left her arms to make the hugging rounds with the others in the room. "Colm?" Gretchen said. "Are you all right with this?"

Colm tugged her back into his arms and Gretchen felt his arm muscles bulge as he tightened his hold on her. He buried his face into her hair almost desperately. She sensed the rawness of his emotion in his grasp and new what concerned him.

"You're going to be a good father, Colm," she whispered her assurance into his ear. "And when your child looks at you, he will see his great big, strong da who could take on the world with one fist tied behind his back and the other lending a helping hand."

Colm sighed. "I see it, Gretchen. Thank you, love. It's going to be all right." He lifted his head and a smile quickly grew. He looked around the room with blatant excitement. "Did you hear? I'm going to be a da! A new home with my beautiful wife, a new job on a wonderful island, and now a new life created by God. When He says He makes all things new, He means it."

Len said, "'Therefore if anyone is in Christ, he is a new creature, the old things passed away. Behold, new things have come.' And speaking of old things." He worked to stand up.

"Len," Gretchen warned, "I told you before I don't want to hear you talking about yourself like that."

Len cackled as he gained his feet slowly. "Not to worry, Gretchen. I'm not going anywhere tonight. In fact, I've got a new baby to look forward to bouncing on my knee, just as I did his mother."

"Wait, did you say 'he'?" Colm jumped in. "Is it a boy? A boy!"

"Whoa, slow down there, Mr. McCrae." Gretchen tugged Colm back to the threshold. "It's way too early to be painting the room blue."

"Blue. I like that. Just like his ma's eyes."

"And his da's."

Colm smiled down at her, but Gretchen indicated with her eyes where some mistletoe hung. One look up and he took his cue.

"Did I ever tell you what my favorite part of the show was?" he asked.

"No. What was it?"

He leaned down, a breath away from her lips. "The part where I would get to say, 'The restoration is complete. But this is not the end of the story.'"

And as was his charming way, even without the camera on him, Colm left Gretchen and all the viewers wanting more.

* * * * *

Dear Reader,

Thank you for joining me on Stepping Stones Island, where the lobster traps are always full and romance awaits even the hardest of hearts. Not that you can blame Gretchen Bauer for guarding her heart so intensely. With the experience she had of someone abusing her goodness, it's only natural to grow wary of letting it happen again—especially with someone who has such a colorful past as Colm McCrae.

And when I say colorful, I mean lots of black and blue. Colm was a new creation in Christ, but he still fought against the anger that once controlled him. As long as it held more power than his belief in God's forgiveness, it would win and keep him down. If it wasn't his past he was fighting, it was the danger to Gretchen that lurked on the island. Colm had his hands full, for sure. At the same time he had a bed-and-breakfast to restore and a heart to win. What a guy!

Thank you for reading *Permanent Vacancy*! I love hearing from readers. Please feel free to contact me to share your thoughts. You can visit my website, www.KatyLeeBooks.com, or email me at KatyLee@KatyLeeBooks.com. If you don't have internet access, you can write to me c/o Love Inspired Books, 233 Broadway, Suite 1001, New York, NY 10279.

Katy Lee